Cloud Watching in the Inferno
Poems & Short Stories — Westley Heine

ROADSIDE PRESS

"Westley Heine keeps reminding me of Sherwood Anderson as I read *Cloud Watching in the Inferno*—as if Anderson had access to a view of the loneliness and rage of current-day America. Heine displays great respect here for humans, for our ability to endure the rottenness of the world and to rage against the minutiae of our suffering. I think of Anderson's "grotesques" for which he had great empathy and created full lives for characters trying to describe or find the ineffable thing they are each missing. Heine has the same empathy and is fighting his way through humanity to show that it's all really terrible and something to celebrate at the same time."—Zak Mucha, LCSW, and author of *Swimming to the Horizon: Crack, Psychosis, and Street-Corner Social Work*

"*Cloud Watching in the Inferno* is searing counterculture literature in this age of extinction. Flip the bluesman a quarter as Heine chronicles tragic and comedic dysfunction along with a dash of hard boiled observations featuring refuges not unlike a shallow grave. There's no escaping, just look into the abyss and smile."—Mike Zone, author of *Skull My Daisy* and *The Earth was Shaking for Days*

"In this writer's collage of poems, short stories, vignettes, and the occasional drawing from fellow artists, Westley Heine takes us through a journey of encounters, people, and places—real, imagined, futuristic, historical, autobiographical, sentimental, visceral, poignant, profane … experiences that refuse easy definition and containment, that seep through cracks, that overflow the edges of what we think we perceive. Get ready—to be moved, to be enlightened, to be educated, to be repulsed, to be delighted, to be provoked—sometimes all at once—by this speaker and his words on this compelling quest to understand the self."—Sarah Rae, author of *Someplace Else*

"*Cloud Watching in the Inferno* is a love-making session gone off the bed into the unknown, where he buries societal expectations of normalcy. It is as refreshing as a cold beer after a long drought encouraged by the nightmare blooming in a Los Angeles fire. Heine's poetry sizzles sharply, cracking the illusion of the soul with sharp visions of colorful reality. Within these pages are the clouds boiling an inferno's intaglio held tenderly in Westley Heine's Milky Way of creation."—Cathleen Schandelmeier, author of *Tattoo Screams of Love* and *Chicago Phoenix*

"The prose voice of "My Old Lady" weaves silly with sincere to get at something true if unfiltered, like mismatched love matches that end as they must. In "Kids These Days" Heine plays with past and present tense brilliantly, in a story about the nature of time and its passing, that reads like Rod Serling by way of Barry Crimmins. His story "Easy Street" may be my favourite prose work of his at this point, rich with imagery and cynicism as it is, like a kind of magic-realism strained through visions of apocalyptic urban sprawl, and hopelessness in unrelenting cyclical existence. "Omega Generation" may be my second favourite, for much the same reasons.

"Some of his stories—like his poems—set in Chicago or in Los Angeles, no matter how involved with showing the lives of the people in them, have that looming feeling the setting is somehow vying to be a scene-stealing character. Occasionally, paying attention to something in a poem enriches the reading experience and understanding of a story later on in the collection, as is true of a story then a poem later.

"The last poem in the collection is one of Heine's best Blues poems ever—"The Devil Is Getting Old." After reading it you will imagine the vocals and rhythm in your mind. If ever a poem was an earworm it is this."—David Alec Knight, author of *LEPER MOSH* and *The Heart is a Hollow Organ*

"Jack Kerouac sought to capture the wild, improvisational beat of jazz in his work. Westley Heine clearly has similar sensibilities—an intuitive sense of phrasing and rhythm. And if you've ever heard him read aloud (often backed by music), this becomes all the more apparent.

"But then there is the simple beauty of the writing. *Cloud Watching* spans surrealist poetry to expertly crafted short stories, often hacking your brain at its depths in some secret code of words ... the haunted and indelible memories of a past love ... or tales of attempting to eke out some meager living writing for a startup mag, and the Gonzo realization that actual life is far more exhilarating than any boring article assignment could ever hope to be ... Another tale impressively resonates with Steinbeck's *Of Mice and Men.* And then another, offering back-alley tinges of Bukowski.

"Some of the stories transcend traditional genre. There is a memorably dark tale of magical-realism that might well have made a classic *Twilight Zone* episode—and with a wonderfully cinematic twist ending. It's the Old West in *Black Mirror* territory.

"Whether it's poetry or prose, Wes's words and style and rhythm are instantly recognizable, in the best ways possible. And there is a wonderfully fitting ending to the collection—detailing a cross-country return to Chicago, the artistic pull of the place, traveling the iconic Route 66, but the reverse direction of so many before. Like a salmon journeying upstream, Heine sought not some mythic western horizon, but returning east from whence he came, toward an artistic procreation in words."—Steven Meleon, author of *St. James Infirmary* and *The Kind the Pharaohs Try*

Table of Contents

Dedicated to

Danielle DeAngelis and Daniel Stine
&
Marie and James Berg
who
gave me a place to crash
when I needed it.

"Midway upon the journey of our life I found myself
within a forest dark."—Dante, *The Inferno*

I See You

I see you in reflections and faces of worn statues
I see you in shoulder glances and flicker between trees
I see you in blurry photos and stains on the tile
I see you in water ripples and in windswept grass
I see you between the lines of poems and in the maze of brain tissue
I see you in broken mirrors and lens flares
I see you in London Bridges and inkblots
I see you in the Mayan Codices and the dust of catacombs
I see you in empty spaces and swarming crowds
I see you in the glimmer of an eye and in the smirk of a joke
I see you in black holes, sun flares, and winking assholes
I see you in wet dreams and waking nightmares
I see you in Rorschach tests and tortillas without the face of Jesus
I see you in reflections on razorblades and imprints on death masks
I see you in sexy Halloween Costumes and pools of oil
I see you in films downloaded from the future
I see you while cloud watching in the Inferno
I see you behind my eyelids as I press them squeezing out the light
I see you for all that you were, you are, and could have been, and will be
I see you, I see you, but I don't want to see you ever again

Honkytonk Angels

Honkytonk Angels spin in a galaxy of rhinestone.
Swirling twirling they dance. As the beer goes flat
as the rain weeps through dank walls.
The singer howls, the pedal steel cries,
drums table-tap codes, the bass beats blood.
Water damaged faces warp, hips dip, stitches strain.
They parade like automatons, but they will it so.

What are their bodies saying in this language without words?
In this silent rhythm? They are the shadows of the music.
Somewhere near seduction they sway, but with the
grace that reminds of religious nobility. Sacred sex?
Divine dancers tangle the question between their legs.
It means everything and nothing. Whale songs. Bird songs.
Mating songs. Spiders wave back at the Milky Way.

There is no meaning except they are alive.
They are not the meaning of life. They are life itself.
Some sweat, hobble, dresses fray like blooming petals.
Tonight they will sleep well, feet and shins worn.
Adrenalin dreams of pairs, squares, spasms, sparks,
glances, glimpses, teeth flash in space.
They are not the question. They are the answer.

Fly

There is a fly in my room.
It does not know how it got in.
It does not know how it will get out.
It does not know what out is,
but it wants out.

I hear its wings
like static between stations.
It changes pitch past my ear.
It lands: a black dot on a white plain.
How maddening it must be to be a larva,
& make the leap to become a fly,
to have wings and a thousand eyes,
but nowhere to soar off to.

He's always at the window
wanting out without knowing what out is.
He throws himself against the glass.
He beats his head against the glycerin.
Kaleidoscope eyes against an
invisible wall of
hard air.
It's bigger than the world he can see.

I wonder if I should set him free?
Should I open the cold glass and pop out the screen?
Should I smash him out of his misery?
Should I play god?

& hope my friend comes back
with thumbs rather than worthless wings?
But it's not that simple…
God, man, or fly he's determined to get through.
My friend throws himself against the glass again & again
until he beats out his brains, until he loses his will.
He falls on his back like dry paper.
He falls there on the windowsill
with a dozen others.

There is a fly in my head.
It does not know how it got here.
It does not know how it will get out, but it
wants to fly out.

My Old Lady

My old lady lived in the building I used to live in off Sheridan Avenue in Uptown Chicago. It was a brown brick hypercube of studio apartments full of retirees, students, bachelors, losers, loners, lovers. My old lady was about five foot two and balding on top. I'm over six foot so it was hot when she would crawl on top of me and ride me as if it was her last time to feel alive. At her age there was always the possibility that it was her last time. She was seventy or eighty but I never found out exactly because she didn't speak English. Also, it would be impolite to ask a lady her age, especially an old lady.

My old lady's eyes disappeared when she smiled. When her lips parted three lone teeth showed. I found more teeth in the back of her mouth. Her forearm was about the size of my average size dick, and had as many blue veins pouring out like tributaries to the delta of her boney hands. When she would grip my shaft it was like a skeleton clinging to the root of life.

My old lady was so old I couldn't tell what race she was. Not that I cared because I'm cool. You know? It's not important because I'm down. You know? Our love wasn't exotic because of racial difference. It was exotic because of the age difference. You know?

My old lady didn't know any tricks from porno movies from the 70s. My old lady didn't know any porno tricks from the 80s. My old lady didn't know any porn tricks from the 90s, 00s, teens, or now. She didn't deep throat, spit, cross her eyes, pop, or slap, or do any of the moves meant to boost a man's fragile ego. Her idea of giving head was to lick me like a snake smelling a pickle. Still, I never pressured her to do anything that would seem unnatural to her. No, I didn't ask her to do anything she would not understand. I never finished on her. She would not find it hot. I sensed she would find it decidedly rude. Instead she would clutch my trusting ass and cling to me like a spider monkey as I emptied my soldiers into her post-menopausal tunnel of light.

My old lady and I met in the laundry room in the basement. She had put in a load of wash into a dryer and was out of quarters. Seeing her pat her pockets, and check her purse over and over I gave her some silver. She smiled up at me and spoke in a language I didn't recognize, but I understood the warm tone. Laundry dry we met again in the elevator. Almost blindly she peered at the numbers on the dial searching for her floor. When we came to her level I held the door open for her. She gripped my bicep and paused. She smiled. She felt up the length of my arm feeling my muscles. She said something in the tone of a joke. I smirked instinctively. She walked into the hall without her laundry bag. Somehow I knew my queue to pick up her bag and carry it to her door. Turning her key she smiled and waved me inside. After some tea she said something in a matter of fact tone and began rubbing my thigh.

That was long ago when she was the same and slightly younger. Now I am much older and never the same. There was something about the way she would moan with abandon unashamed of pleasure and unashamed of life. She would dirty talk completely unconcerned that I didn't understand what she was saying. There was something real about her nipples chewed by children. There was something vital in her taut muscles strained by a life of labor. There was something in the way she would quiver impaled on me, her whole body lifted in my arms, floating in the air, tears silently falling down her cheeks.

Though it was non-verbal it wasn't all physical. Sometimes after we'd make it she'd put on old jazz records and we'd dance slowly across her lattice of throw rugs. As she would talk down into herself I'd stare over her shoulder out the window at the moon. Sometimes she would cook. Sometimes I would show up with take out. Whenever I would start to nod off in bed she would slap my beer belly, flick her hand at me gesturing me off the bed, and brushing me out the door to my own room where we would both sleep better alone. At the door I would lean in to kiss her goodnight but she would just laugh, pinch my cheeks, and say something, nothing, everything.

Finally, it occurred to me that I might make a gesture to show her that she was more than just a fuck-buddy. I went down to the corner and along with my usual purchase of a six pack and a pint of dark rum I pointed to a bouquet of blue flowers wrapped in a plastic sheath. Feeling good I galloped down the sidewalk the petals fluttering away in the wind like butterflies. I danced through the lobby and hit the button for the elevator. At my old lady's floor I saw the landlord by her door.

He chewed his unlit cigar. He eyed me up and down. When he saw the posies his pupils popped. "You're early kid."

"Early?"

He removed the cigar from his mouth to enunciate

and spit a strand of loose tobacco on the green carpet. "I mean with those flowers… You're early for the funeral."

The landlord smirked.

I hung my head.

In the corner of my eye I could see in the open door. The undertaker was there dressed in black. He might have well been the Grim Reaper.

My arm came up and I handed the landlord my bouquet of blue flowers. I turned around and marched back to the elevator.

"What the fuck am I supposed to do with these?" he grumbled over the back of my spine. My ears turned hot and red.

In my room I cracked a beer. I sipped the rum straight from the bottle. I didn't have any ice. She always kept ice.

Maybe it was the booze, but I began to think the gesture with the flowers was more for me than it was for her. She comforted me during the cold winter nights. She accepted me when women my own age wouldn't even talk to me. My old lady didn't need to talk to me at all. She would have laughed at my flowers. She probably would have patted me on the arm and pitied me. I wondered how many times in her long life she had been in love? She knew how it is. She knew how it goes. She would have crooned in her strange language over the flowers like she did over my manhood every time I couldn't get hard, or came too quick, or couldn't cum at all but trusted endlessly and hopelessly towards an ever receding dawn. She would tap out like a tired wrestler, pucker her lips, and moan a sorrowful joke over our futile dance.

In the lobby there was a flier for the funeral services on the bulletin board. It was there so the landlord didn't feel so cold about running affordable housing for those at the end of their lives and those at the beginning of their lives. When I saw it I took down the information.

At the funeral I saw my old ladies' children for the first time. She didn't have pictures of them in her room. They didn't seem sad. They dressed as fancy as possible in contrast to my old lady's simple style from her modest era. I could tell they had little cultural connection to her. By looking at them I could finally see what race my old lady was. Not that I cared what race she was because I'm cool. You know? It's not important because I'm down. You know? But her children seemed disturbed by my presence. They looked over their shoulders and grumbled at me. Still, I couldn't tell if they knew I was their mother's lover and resented me, or if they didn't like the way I dressed in my dirty jacket and torn slacks. I suppose they thought I was crashing the funeral home for the dry cookies and watery coffee.

My old lady didn't leave me any money. I'm sure she didn't have any. Nor did I want any. I would have been happy with a couple records from her jazz collection. My old lady didn't hold any expectations about our time together. My old lady didn't expect anything from me. My old lady didn't expect me to love her. My old lady didn't expect me to take care of her. My old lady didn't know my name. But from the flier on the bulletin board funeral I learned her name.

My old lady's name was: Ona. So now after midnight I moan, "Ona. Ona. Ona. Ona!"

Kids These Days

Ricky Foyle patrolled/patrols the streets of Hollywood even slept/sleeps outside manning his post always keeping/keeps one eye on the sky. He wore/wears a purple wig, a Starter jacket, and sunglasses when he could/can find them. His cover served/serves its purpose. Searchlights waved/wave in the sky signaling above the palm trees.

"This town is a launch. It's a launch pad. You don't see'em. They travel at the speed of light. When you travel at the speed of light you don't see the light."

As he walked/walks he spoke/speaks out loud. He narrated/narrates reality to keep all the moving parts straight. There were/are many players. He was/is sure he's being recorded by all cellphones, traffic cams, the humming telephone poles, dogs with cameras in their eyes, two-way TVs, people pretending to take a selfie but really recording him. That's good he thought/thinks. He wasn't/isn't afraid of them. Not anymore. He had/has to get the word out. If he didn't/don't report out loud, all the outside signals would/will penetrate him. Ricky's only shield was/is the truth.

"Kids these days… they're older than us. You know time dilation? If you travel at the speed of light you're going faster than time down here on Earth. You cruise say ten years in space and come back home and it's a thousand years later here on Earth. Wait, carry the one… a Jesus freak stole my charts… But you get back and everyone's gone. Everything's changed. Well, most things."

"I took one ride. Wanted to see Saturn. Come back and my parents don't recognize me, my sister replaced by a sex doll. Figured that they are long dead. It gets lonely here in the future."

It was/is dark. The streetlights along Santa Monica Boulevard glowed/glow orange like jack-o-lanterns. On the corner of Normandie two transgender souls gestured/gesture to the cars at the stoplight. One wearing plastic cat ears and vampire fangs leaned/leans up to a black SUV. "Get it giiiiiirl," snarled/snarls her friend.

"Kids these days don't have any respect for time. Why should they? They come and go as they please… a thousand years here… a thousand years there… All they care about is cruising… getting their jollies warping the continuum… Speeding they call it… all they care about is space. They don't care about us down here keeping time, maintaining history, keeping the shops open, fighting off wars, pollution, electromagnetic info fields, sound cannons... Yeah, they don't care. They pull into Hollywood like a drive-in movie, suck up some energy and go. That's this town's number one export: light projections."

Ricky entered/enters the 24 hour Laundromat. It was/is warm inside. The attendant was/is a stout Mexican lady folding some sheets for pick-up. She paused and wiped/wipes her hands on her apron. She didn't/doesn't understand Ricky's monologue but she didn't/doesn't like the sound of it. Ricky could/can feel her watching him. When a customer put/puts a five-dollar bill in the change machine and the quarters dropped/drop Ricky mimicked/mimics the transaction. He pretended/pretends to put a bill in the machine. No coins dropped/drop but he swooped/swoops them up anyway. No one inside had/has a cigarette. When the attendant gave/gives him the eye he left/leaves.

"It's hard down here in time. Gotta find something to eat, gotta find a place to sleep, gotta look out for the robo-dogs. It's all to keep you distracted. Kids, they have no respect for time. They bypass it. After one trip, two trips, soon there are all these different strands of history… there are so many timelines that time itself becomes meaningless. Kids these days have no respect… they leave the continuum in shreds…"

As the sun rose/rises above Santa Monica Boulevard the night dissolved/dissolves into long shadows that panned/pan and finally shrunk/shrink into the day. Legions of souls dragging airport bags on wheels began/begin their march. But they weren't/ aren't going to the airport. They weren't/ aren't going anywhere. They wandered/wander to stay warm. They came/come from all over. L.A. was/is the end of the road in America.

"Funny thing is, kids have the advanced technology to go the speed of light, but they have been in space so long that when they come back they act like country cousins. They first left what? Some negative year B.C? All the numbers are made up anyway… But they act like hicks… No manners… standing on the corner scratching ass, mouths open drool hanging to the curb, kicking the tires of the cars, poking at ladies grinning and sniffing their fingers, screaming in horror at the sight of a neon sign, bursting into tears at the sound of music. They're always talking about how the pyramids used to be smooth and shiny and we let them get run down. Or how England used to be cool, everyone painting themselves blue and up all night sacrificing virgins, but now just a bunch of stiff sticks in the mud sipping tea through wooden teeth."

"Kids these days… bunch of pinheads cross-eyed from the time warp, half blind from the blackness beyond the speed of light, boneless but propped up in their gravity suits. Nothing but a bunch of slack-jawed cavemen pillaging our cities like space-Vikings, running into the pawnshop with a golden chalice from ancient Mesopotamia leaving with only a thousand bucks just to cross the street and blow it all at Krispy Crème. Ever see them? No. You wouldn't. You know how you watch an old movie and they're speaking English, but they don't make much sense? They're like that. But these kids are so old most people don't even see them. If you do, you don't want to see them. They have milky blue eyes from space blindness. Gravity suits warp their features and they gurgle and spit out the sides of their mouths as they talk. Digging through trashcans looking for fuel, jacking off in the middle of a shopping mall, crapping in the middle of the street. Dumping ballast they call it."

Ricky turned/turns north on Western Avenue. The cars growled/growl like tigers. As he crossed/crosses the bridge over Hwy 101 Ricky looked/looks down at the river of steel.

"Kids these days… I gotta look out. Don't want them taking me into space again. No sir. If they scoop me up, who knows how long I'd be? Get back and it's the year three thousand or some shit… Only thing I know is that as time goes on things get better for some people and worse for others. No use fooling. I ain't no little tramp. I'm a student of physics. I ain't no jockstrap. I'm one of the others. Civilization gets so bad it tears itself apart and things start over again. Over and over… There's many histories. Most are erased. Forgotten. Don't wanna remember anyhoo… Don't wanna come back from space during a down cycle and be surrounded by rubble and cannibals…"

"Shit. Kids come out of the time warp and refuel at the movies. Going to the flickers they call it. Taking a light bath they say. Recharges the pineal gland. Once they get their light fix they hotrod back into the blackness and back to dreaming at the speed of light. It's a real high eyeballing at the edge of a light beam. Punks. Spacetime punks. No respect for time. No respect for history. No respect for progress. Right now is a good time on Earth. It's the land of plenty. People throw out what they don't need. Food is for the picking."

In one of the dead end streets cut off by the freeway Ricky knew/knows a place where he could/can lay low on some cardboard under some shade. He squeezed/squeezes through a hole in a chain link fence and walked/walks on the worn path along the embankment.

"It was in Hawaii Hendrix saw the aliens. Lost trails in the rainbow blur from Fuji. Color photos in the chemical burn. A smile takes its own picture flashing the skull in such a way. It's an x-ray to see if you're ripe. Lose your bones in space. Don't need'em. Weightless up there you know. Use my excess skin to scoop up electrons and fly like a Ram-jet. When you can go anywhere in the universe you realize there is nowhere to go. Everywhere is nowhere. So I went back home. That's the kicker. When I got back the planet I grew up on was gone. That's the only place you can't go. You can't go back. You can't go home."

Zen In Hell

1
Fearfully in danger
my heart is emptied
into the arena.

Digested dreams plop on stage the crowd claws forth.
From a wall of white noise the ego grins behind the
curtain as the subconscious does a striptease
bathing in holy light.
Molded by intestines, beaten into
shape by natives from local spacetime
expunged with a mirror mask and nudes at the window.

Have a tryst with memory.
Temporary pleasure seeds the future forever.
Accusations chirp like crickets.
Staggering to the next life.
Blacked out, the phantom finally un-masked,
forgotten in the morning.

In exile we dance
in fire flickers and rum rubbed hips.
Boyhood dreams harden into a mask of smiles
locking the heart into a cement skull.

2
Man-plant
Vicious sun
Flower of eyes
Pores popping seeds
Lead by primordial instincts
Ape king pulls us on a cape of entrails
Tits hang in galleries
Ghosts lead on chains

You can steal the silver
You can cut the cord
You can sell your hair in the street,
but no escape from a circle.

Sexual pilgrim visits exotic lands under
an umbrella of petals
crawling on knees to the flesh altar.
Bazaar dung-beetle gods dance outside the city walls
offering nuts and pumpkins clutched in claws.
Deal sealed in the tavern where
we walk on the ceiling.
Smuggled in a coffin.
Excused by magic tricks.
Brain replaced by crystal ball.
Grinning like the sun
toasting our manes
selling personas
brides groomed
seashells snatched
on a bed of snakes we play piggyback

a bloodletting of love
bobbing for skulls
punished with pleasure
edited by time
sleeping with statues
intentions buried like fossils
found by chance
echoed by survivors
dictated by folly

3
Catastrophe: tectonics collapse
ice shelves hemorrhage
a goddess breaks her heel
train wrecks, London bridges, clocks flooded
Milky Way legs kick can-can
a tidal wave of curtains
drowning in dreams
birthed by storm
conjuring chaos
hysterical hysteria
washed up in
sterile lies and
Cinderella cinders.
Ideals float away like fireflies.

4
The past hung a symbol above our heads.
Wrap our hair in cloth.
Cover our nakedness with dragons.
Shame our pride in a bundle of walls.

I'd rather stand naked in the fire.
I'd rather expose myself to the white light.
I'd rather be publically humiliated in the
stocks kicked in the ass by juvenile jokes

than shamed behind the curtain
than cowed by merchants with scorpion tails
than pricked by peepholes.
I'd rather commit suicide sliding down the bannister
than revived by hot air.

We pray to our own wings.
We make up our minds by making up our minds.
We create the painting on the wall by interpreting it.
In waiting rooms we take Heaven for granted
counting desires rather than blessings.

As the wallpaper talks we cast nets across the stars.
The universe is a violent place of fire and power all
candles in the void.
The Earth is wet with anticipation.

This is the new art, the automatic art.
Projectors machinegun.
We read the music.

We paint by number.
We green light by formula.
We cast by caste.
We pan for gold in a cesspool.
We kiss the smoke.
The universal truth
is our little secret.

5
A fresh one falls into the salt mine.
Shadows move from the walls.
We writhe in the purple light.
A new one drops white & tender.
Her milky skin wet with birth broth not ripe for long.
We circle and claw. She begins to bake.
We chew and lick. She begins to cook.
Before her eyes adjust she is crucified in missionary.
Soon skin a lattice of scars, a map of memories, flesh
tanned vermillion.
Open sores, pieces of genitals like flayed flags,
eyes black hungry for light,
teeth sharpened by life, pacing on fingernails long as
stilts
she takes her place among us.

Banished butterfly
Plucked angel
Bald vulture
Doomed to scavenge outside the prison
No longer forcefed bullets
Hanging by tails

Hung by entrails
Spiraling in depths of oily feathers
Grappling with breasts
Foot holes in cunt
Stepping stones of cock
Tortured by tickle
Demon seed burns the throat
A freakshow selling normal
Bloodshot wings weighed down by pleasure
Where is the Exodus from this pyramid scheme?
From slave gods and field hollers?
As weasels nibble the brain of the Sphinx.
As workers hoist their children like flags.
They will step on your throat in the garden of skulls.

6
Well, well, well…
Kick over your Magic 8 Ball.
Count your eggs.
Stop singing your duel.
Hung like a piñata exploding
like Heaven raining blood we are
blindfolded to the stick in our hands.
I'd rather be an open casket.

Shadow Boxing in Uptown

A fourteen-year-old boy raises his fists at me. I get down on one knee. His hands are taped up. He's wearing an undershirt with an Everlast logo. Sweat is pouring from his scalp, which is buzzed into a fade. As I snap his picture his eyes flash a look of innocence. Then fearlessness. Are they the same thing? Through the lens I see things that might not have been there before. Is it life experience that makes so many old folks afraid of everything? Is it ignorance that makes youngsters so unafraid of life, so unafraid of death?

I'm not getting paid for this. Neither is he. I'm an intern at a boxing magazine in Chicago. When I came into the community center he didn't ask who I was. He just saw the camera and instinctively popped into a stance. After the camera snaps, the kid smiles past the mouth guard, nods, and sheds his pose. He goes back to slamming the bag, which is patched up with duct tape. Obviously, he's done this before. I haven't.

I overhear Logan, the publisher of the magazine, talking to the coach who runs the community center. Today the place serves as a gym for these young aspiring gladiators. There's chipped green paint on the wall. The Mexican and American flag are proudly displayed side by side. The coach in a tight white t-shirt crosses his arms standing firm as a statue. He is saying boxing is keeping these kids off the street and fighting in gangs. Hearing this my brain offers a hollow ironic quip about how some kids don't have much of a choice: fight inside or fight outside. But I don't say anything because I know I'm wrong. This is a good alternative. Every one of these kids knows they can make stacks of cash hustling pills and powder on the corners, but they run the risk of getting busted, getting robbed, or getting killed. Here in the ring any prize money is years of hard work and luck away. At least boxers fight fair man to man, fist to fist, and don't hide behind a gun. The worst that can happen to a fighter is his brains get scrambled. But that's only if they go pro and get exploited night after night. Let's face it. The underworld has its hooks in professional boxing as much as it does in the dope game. Only the mortality rate is lower in the ring. Most of the kids here won't go pro. They are sparring just for exercise like any other sport.

Yet I don't know much about sports. Never have. I've never been much of a jock. I just want to be a writer. You have to start somewhere. So I answered this ad on Craigslist for an internship. How in the hell am I going to get Logan to let me write a story when I can't even adhere to the oldest writer cliché in the book: write what you know. Guess I'll have to learn.

After I send Logan the pics I took at the community center he decides to have me come along on his next outing. There's a weigh-in taking place on North Beach. I don't think it's the quality of my photography that makes Logan keep me around. Besides working for free, I only live a few blocks away from his place in Uptown. The real reason is that it gives Logan some clout walking into an event with an assistant, a lackey trailing behind him with the tripod and sweating from drinking too much the night before. The alarm clock rings me into a hung over headache. Without time to shower I hoof it to his place.

Uptown Chicago 2004: Churches, fast-food joints, rich Zen gardens with drunks sitting outside the walls. The Baptist Mission, Rick's Records, The Green Mill Jazz & Cocktail Lounge. Halfway houses, pizza by the slice, the smokers stomping butts outside the Methadone clinic. Young professionals jog by with the sounds of the apocalypse plugged into their skulls. The twitching hips of radioactive pimps leaping under lampposts. Old women carrying bags full of dusty past lives. Meth addicts with accelerated life spans hit senility at thirty and drift utterly confused. A traffic jam on Lake Shore Drive honks the national anthem.

Most of Uptown is made of brown brick buildings lost in a noir 1940s time warp. Logan lives in one of the new plastic condos walled off from the rest of the world. Passing the JJ Peppers Liquor Store I frequent I come to his complex. The old boys juicing in the afternoon sunshine sit on the wall separating the manicured Zen of the gated community that divides one reality from keeping it real. He buzzes me in.

Waving from the top of the stairs Logan greets me. His mustache bends with his polite smile. He keeps his balding head neatly shaved. He always dresses in tight black clothes carefully chosen to never go out of style. He works out religiously trying to stay young and competitive in the nightlife. He's a handsome old gent except for the turkey wattle dangling from his gullet, which only remains because they haven't invented an exercise to tighten the throat yet. He's unmarried, in his mid-fifties, and in passing I have learned he comes from money. Yet, it's always been his dream to make his own fortune. The boxing magazine is his latest venture. Right now we're gathering material for the first issue.

His apartment is kept in a chic minimalist style: the hardwood floor, black leather furniture, tasteful prints squared away in black frames. Most of the artwork on the walls is his own: the two book covers he did for Stephen King back in the 80s, a Photoshop creation of a demon whose skin is made of dollar bills as if to imply that money is evil, though he never had to suffer the evils of living without it.

I ask obvious questions to make small talk. He explains his home gym equipment as I yawn and rub my beer belly. He shows me the magazine he is modeling the boxing magazine after. It's a small four-inch by five-inch rag called Scene. It hypes which clubs are trendy downtown or in the neighborhoods gentrified enough for tourists, businessmen, or suburban dwellers making day trips into the core of Chicago. It's full of color photos of scantily clad bartenders and waitresses who are just trying to hustle for tips in these fabulous sweaty furnaces where those out-to-be-in flush their funds. This magazine we are modeling our layout after is hand held. It seems far too small for a sports publication, but what do I know? He's the boss.

Logan looks up from Scene and says, "Did I tell you I know R. Kelly?" He has, but I say no trying to hide the fact that I don't care. I don't like pop music. This is before it came out R. Kelly was pissing on minors. "Sometime I'll take you to Coyote Ugly." I think: wasn't there a shitty film about that place? I wonder if the one in Chicago was before or after the B-movie. I nod and change the subject, doubting more and more I'll ever get my first writing credit from working at this startup.

Finally Logan senses the awkward pauses. We wrap the lanyards containing the press passes he Photoshopped himself around our necks and head out. Still in the parking garage he puts on his Blue-Blocker Sunglasses and we crawl into his Jaguar. Only using transit in the city, I haven't been in a car in months. The inertia drags and slams at my hungover body. I'm starting to get the impression he's doing it on purpose to show off. He speeds up after every stop sign and slams on the brakes before the next one. Maybe his car is too fast for the road. Finally on Lake Shore Drive we're free from the grid and start flying. The teeth of the city line the right and the endless blue of Lake Michigan sparkles on the left.

Just off the bike path at North Beach there is a small section roped off for the weigh-in. Logan and I flash our homemade press passes. I'm sweating and staggering through the sand. Logan leaps ahead. There's a small crowd mostly made of other media as well as haggard old boxing judges, promoters, and cigar chomping gamblers. Some of these old timers seem from another era. It's as if they haven't seen the light of day in decades wearing dusty little hats, suspenders, and squinting in the sun as if lost in the flash of a time warp. Despite the heat some are shrouded in skin toned trench coats like dirty old men that have been lost in a maze of subterranean Times Square peep shows before emerging here on the sun soaked beach.

Two large scales are pitted against each other like Rock'em Sock'em Robots. A little man with a greasy combover begins talking. Without a microphone his words are lost in the Chicago wind. Then the first boxer comes out donned in a red silk robe. Stepping up to the scale he drops the robe revealing his oiled, olive, muscular body. All the cameras start snapping like excited insects. The old timers clap, cheer, and grunt in approval. The fighter is being weighed like a healthy piece of man meat at market. The little man announces the weight. Everyone nods in approval and jots it down on notepads. The man next to me licks his lips. "Hot?" he smirks out the side of his mouth.

"What?" I eye him.

"Hot out here ain't it?"

"Oh," realizing he means the weather. "Sure is. Wish I brought some water."

Stepping down from the scale the young fighter poses before the cameras. He flexes, grins, and sticks out his pink tongue. It's as if that fourteen-year-old kid in the gym the other day has grown up. There is no longer a look of innocence and fearlessness. There's no longer a steely look of daft seriousness. He is hamming it up. Clowning. He's a professional. Like a streetwalker who's lost all sense of mystery he throws back his head and laughs. A gold tooth flashes in the sun.

The next fighter emerges and the process repeats. The homoerotic overtones aside, everyone seems to be having a good time. Nothing wrong with a little homoerotica, but since it remains curtained in the ceremony of the sport it makes it seem dirty, closeted, cowardly. The next muscular young man at the peak of his powers steps off the scale, and apparently he's made the grade as well. Everyone claps at the beautiful boy. The shame of appreciating his youthful vitality won't last long. The old vampires milling around wrapped in trench coats like dried wings are collectively willing him to fight until bloody, fight until his features warp, until he ain't pretty no more. Ten, fifteen years he'll be another pummeled putty faced old man with cauliflower ear and just slow-witted enough to be likeable. There won't be any more flashes of repressed homosexual urges looking at that mug. Maybe he'll finally let his muscles lax and his gut hatch forth, but ashamed enough to wrap it in a trench coat and hide the cuts on his eyebrows in the shadow of a fedora. Then he'll be one of them.

Back in Uptown Logan needs to drum up some advertising for the magazine. Like most media a magazine makes the bulk of its money from selling ad space, not from subscriptions or the purchase price of the rag itself. Since we're new it's going to be hard work. No one has heard of us. Logan sets up a desk in the back room of his condo. He plugs in a phone and brings me a list of every boxing gym and martial arts studio in Chicago. He wants me to call them one by one and see if they're willing to buy ad space. It's a nightmare. Most of the gyms don't answer. If they do it's attitude first questions later. The Do Jo's at the martial arts studios don't understand much English and once they get the gist of what I'm asking they'd rather karate chop me than buy ad space. A to Z I go through them all. I make zero sales. I'm no salesman. I'm not competitive. Maybe if there were a commission involved I would have tried harder.

Still, Logan appreciates the effort. He says he'll finally bring me to a fight. If I write an article on the bout he says he'll read it. Meanwhile he says he knows where Don King is partying tonight and he's going to try and hunt the famous promoter down for an interview.

A few days later I'm standing at the corner of Sheridan and Wilson between the boarded up Burger King and the Baptist Church. I have my camera, notepad, and a handheld tape recorder. When Logan pulls up I crawl into his Jaguar. He has the talk radio station on… loud. I think: please why don't you put on some rock and roll? Politically Logan and I see eye to eye. This is the Bush years: two wars, Enron, the economy teetering. There's plenty to be mad about. But I rather not wallow in it.

Logan adds his commentary about the broadcaster's commentary. "Anytime someone uses the word folks they are trying to sell you something." Finally he turns it off and asks me, "So, which writers do you like?"

I have the short list loaded in my head. I begin, "I like Hunter S. Thompson…"

"He's insane!" Logan interrupts.

I think: Yeah, a little bit. That's what makes him fun to read. There's nothing more tiresome than good sense.

I change the subject. "Did you find Don King?"

Logan smiles. "Look in the glove compartment."

Inside is a stack of color prints. There is Don King posed with his spikey grey hair, gold rings, chains, grinning away waving two miniature American flags like sparklers on the Fourth of July.

"That's going to be the cover."

"Good for you man."

"Good for me? Good for us."

I think people would rather see the sport in action than Don King's mug on the cover. King is a flashy pimp who because of his loud personality and slick business exploits has managed to become a D-list celebrity. He's everything that is wrong with boxing: the hype over substance, and the money getting in the way of the real contenders. He's Las Vegas personified. Having him on the cover sends the wrong message. It's as if we are standing in his corner waving the towel in his sweaty face.

"How was the interview?"

"There's a transcript under the prints."

I scan the convo. It's filled with the buzzwords King uses to deflect questions just like a politician. "Only in America!" is printed over and over. It's a Xerox of the caricature he created for himself. It's not far from the depiction of him in The Simpsons. There's no evidence of the real man. There are no hard questions asked. I suppose Logan didn't want to burn any bridges during the first issue of the magazine. Be careful which bridges you cross.

Putting the bundle back in the glove Logan expertly navigates the tunnels of Lower Wacker Drive circumventing The Loop and downtown traffic. Soon we are soaring on I-55 veering off into the South Side.

We arrive at a large banquet hall on Archer Avenue. There's a banner hanging from the door. The name of the event is Latin Fire. I examine the flier. Ten Hispanic men without shirts and arms crossed are Photoshopped in high gloss. The words Latin Fire have purple flames wrapped around them.

Inside the ring floats on stale air and is bathed in fluorescent lights. Beer is being served through a window at the far end of the hall. Bleachers are set up where spectators sip their suds. Logan leaps forward and stakes out a spot ringside to take close-ups of the action. Once he's out of sight I ease over to the window. All they have is Bud and Corona. Beer in hand I find a spot on the back wall where I can see everything.

Sweating in his tux the announcer does his "Ready to Rumbleeeeeeeeee!" speech. I flip on my hand held tape recorder where I mumble what I see. I don't know what I'm talking about but I give my commentary anyway. They start with the featherweights, then the lightweights, next the welterweights. A pattern begins to emerge. Each pairing of fighters is a Hispanic guy fighting a white or black guy. In each bout the Latino fighter always wins.

Only one fight is close. The judges have to get up to deliver their decision to the ref. One old judge is too tall for his own good. He pushes himself up with a cane where he teeters forward like a giant praying mantis, his jaw dangling under his long face. His spectacles slip down his barren brow finally reaching the edge of his nose where he examines his score sheet of tallied punches and errors. The decision is in. The Latin fighter's arm is raised and the crowd cheers.

Soon I stop recording my commentary for the story I'm supposed to be writing. My words were just an endless stream of: "Oh... Wow... Left hook... Right jab... Ouch... There's some blood..." I am more interested in the crowd: Old Mexican men in white cowboy hats sipping Corona from plastic cups squint at the ring... Young Mexican men with backwards baseball caps laughing, cheering, clawing the air... Mustaches wet with beer. The stoic judges with potato faces. Leather expressions. Bald spots haloed in curls. The only women present are the two card girls. Between each round they take turns carrying a large placard: Round 1, Round 2, etc. Teetering on high heels they parade across the bloody ring in blue bikinis hipbones protruding, toothpaste commercial smiles, ribs you could scrub your wash on. Tanned, shaved, and sterilized they grit their teeth. The men in the crowd hoot and whistle in celebration of their anorexia.

I have to admit it's a lively scene. The ring grows stained like a dirty bathtub. The air fills with more blue smoke. The ground gets sticky with beer. The bloodlust is palatable after one Hispanic fighter after another beats the shit of their white or black opponents. Loose teeth are sent flying across the room. A kid is collecting them like a ball boy at a tennis match. He assembles the pearly whites into necklaces, which he sells in the parking lot afterwards.

The main event is announced. The heavyweight fight begins. The fight is so one-sided the Latin boxer is waving his gloves at his opponent like, "Come on, try and punch me." He puts his hands down. He ceases to defend himself, but the black fighter in the blue shorts still refuses to charge. Like a Spanish Sun God the Latino heavyweight in the red shorts dances in circles. He turns his back to the other fighter. He mocks the other boxer.

I stop taking notes. I stop my tape recorder. I lean against the wall and take it all in. Something is not right here. I'm surprised how much race seems to be involved. I have nothing against anybody, in fact I love Latino culture, but the whole event is just an excuse for people to watch fighters of their own race beat up white and black guys. It's a racial pride thing. Latin Fire indeed. It all seems rigged. One after the other each fight is one-sided. Nothing is that perfect. No one seems to notice. No one seems to care.

In the car heading back to the North Side Logan asks me what I think. I can't think of a way to bring up race without feeling afraid of sounding racist. So I don't say anything. I don't want him to take it the wrong way. As I am still choosing my words he changes the subject. "There's an up and coming fighter I think you should interview. You seem stuck for a subject to write about. He won a string of a dozen fights, but suddenly lost the last three. See if you can find out what's up."

Back at Logan's condo he pulls up a website and shows me the fighter in question. It's an action shot of a young black guy swinging towards the camera. His teeth are bared. His eyes are fierce. He actually seems to want to hurt the cameraman. His name is Kareem "The Viper" Vance. "He trains down in Gary Indiana, but when he's in town sometimes he uses a gym on the West Side. Carrie is another freelance writer working on something. You could drive with her."

Carrie is a real writer. Everyone can tell she's a writer because she wears a scarf and a little hat. Her glasses dangle on a neon string. Despite the uniform she has some real Chicago grit to her. She holds her own with the boxers and all the testosterone junkies in the gyms spitting into buckets. She has a hell of a lot of writing credits while I have zero. Maybe I should get a little hat.

We buzz around in her Honda staking out the gyms around town. She lets me use her cell phone to call the training facility in Gary where Kareem "The Viper" Vance works out. No one answers. Carrie is encouraging. She actually listens to me when I talk about writers I like. She's impressed that I read my stuff at the Green Mill in Uptown, home of the original Poetry Slam where the crowd is encouraged to hiss, boo, and stomp if a poet is being pretentious.

Finally the place in Gary Indiana answers the phone. There's some static at first but I confirm that Kareem is there. A voice comes on telling me he's the Viper's manager. Kareem will be there until five. If we come now he'll wait for us and do the interview.

As we climb the Skyway arching over the smokestacks I use a stack of printouts from MapQuest to direct Carrie through the industrial zones and strip malls that make up Gary. Finally we arrive at the training facility. It's a windowless white hanger. I ring the buzzer. I knock on the steel door. I call the phone number. Crickets. It's only four p.m. They said they'd wait. I put my ear to the door and listen for movement. Nothing. Everyone has left. We've been stood up. It's a cold overcast day in Gary Indiana.

"Who's the fighter Logan wanted you to interview again?"

"The Viper or some shit. Kareem Vance."

"Oh. He was hot, but now he's on a losing streak right?"

"That's what Logan said."

"Sometimes when they avoid interviews it's because a fighter has become punch-drunk. They don't want you to talk to him because they don't want it made public that his brains are scrambled."

"Damn."

I think of the promo picture Logan showed me of the young fighter. There was something off about the look in his eyes. He wasn't posing. There was fire in his eyes and he was charging the camera. Either way we drove all this way for nothing. By the time we get back to Chicago it's getting dark. Carrie drops me off at the Red Line and wishes me luck.

Without the interview I don't know what I'm going to write. Back in Uptown I stop in at JJ Peppers and grab a six pack of Old Style. I come out of my own thoughts for a minute when the friendly middle-eastern clerk suddenly leaps over the counter with a baseball bat. Before I know what's happening he's chasing a kid through the parking lot. When he returns he smiles and explains it was a shoplifter. Before turning towards my place I peer up at Logan's condo. I imagine one of the lights on the stubborn plastic tower is his window where he is awaiting my copy.

Soon I'm pacing in my studio apartment trying to write a story, any story for the magazine. I begin bouncing on my heels. The floor shakes. The light bulb hanging from the ceiling sways. Occasionally I return to the keyboard and crunch a line. I am trying to punch out the word, the hype, to find the humanity in this sport, which seems to exist in its own vacuum. It has its own rules, its own morality. Where is the lifeblood under these posing, dancing, jabbing forms? These silhouettes spare like paper dolls and shadow puppets. Where does the ring stop and life begin? It's getting hard to tell. As I crack another beer I try to get the feel of it in my bones. I shoot my fists forward. Shadows streak across the wall like spawning eels. I cut the air. The light bulb sways more violently. The room spins like a Zoetrope. I hammer my knuckles forward like pistons. My arms tear out of the sockets. I sock the wall one, two, three. My neighbor on the other side pounds back one, two, three. Life is all around.

The ring is in this room. The ring is out on the corner where the dealers dispense their dust. The ring is at JJ Peppers where the clerk leaps over the counter with a baseball bat chasing a shoplifter. The ring is in The Loop downtown where the waking world sells their time for money. There are many rings to this hell. The rings move around each other like a delicate clock. They dance in circles like two prizefighters sizing each other up. The rings all accrete to something. They spiral towards something. There is a center somewhere. There is a core. There is a point. It's at the tip of my tongue. It's between the words.

How in the hell am I going to write a story when I can't even adhere to the oldest writer cliché in the book: write what you know. I don't know anything… No one does. No one knows anything. Anyone who says otherwise is giving you a line, is selling something folks, posing for a camera with fists up… all bullshit until the real fight begins. Only then do we see what we're made of. People might cling to beliefs, over simplified principles, but no one really knows a damn thing about life. There is only the mystery, the bells in the night, the clocks getting rung, the skulls knocking together. There's the bell… and they're off… Round one, two, three, until you can't take it anymore and you're down for the count, leaping up again, and down again… your tongue across the mat. But the ref keeps counting above your unconscious body ten, nine, eight, seven… knock out… six, five, four… I crack another beer… blackout…. I keep typing… three, two, one… lift off!

Church bells in the night and alarm clocks in the morning… So many clichés in the book, and there is a book for writers. Odd thing is: the book is unwritten. It's full of unwritten rules like: never turn in a piece of sports journalism about yourself. So in the hungover morning after I turn in this story, the rough draft of the story you're reading now, it's rejected. Due to my cruel observations about him Logan doesn't speak to me again. But it doesn't matter. Not long after the first issue the magazine folds. Turns out no one wanted to see that cartoon gangster Don King on the cover. After that Logan packed it in. For all his macho posing Logan had feelings. Last I heard he moved to Thailand where being a dirty old man was cheaper and easier. I wouldn't get anything in print for years.

Is it life experience that makes so many old folks afraid of everything? Is it ignorance that makes youngsters so unafraid of life, so unafraid of death? No. It's a good line but it's not that simple. It can go either way. People are made of different stuff. As life doles out its punches some grow harder. Some become tenderized. No matter who you are, life will beat the shit out of you eventually. Everyone gets their bell rung in the end. It's just some old timers flinch. Some lean in and absorb the punch. We all get a little punch-drunk with time. We all get a little batty round after round. Meanwhile the bell keeps ringing.

Bullfight at the Supermarket

Every time we bite, chew, and swallow it's a sacrifice.
(Wide eyes of innocent animals crucified.)
Every time we breathe in and out it's a sacrifice.
(Vegetation resuscitates the world as we plow it under.)

In each breath there's a crucifixion.
If you open your arms
If you open your eyes
your legs
your mouth
you are at once guilty and innocent.
Guilty by consuming and
innocent by the need to consume.
Flowers grown and flowers picked
sacrificed and sanctified
crucifying and crucified
living to die
dying to live
until words are twilight.

The devil is released into the arena.
Before the crowd the priests spar with the beast.
Spears shish kabob, vales blindfold,
horns pulled back revving in submission.
Slaughtered by a double-edged sword the masses cheer.
They have been saved from nature once again.
They give a standing ovation on two legs above it all
for now.

One thing for another
bullfights and fur coats
steak dinners and leather jackets
rib cages and wings
breasts and twins
lungs and lyrics
eclipsed by metaphors and symbols but
the crucifixion is everywhere.

Shot of Mercy

The horizon cracked purple and dawn spilled across the dewed hills of Tennessee. Paul McKenzie was cleaning his double barrel shotgun. He sat on the porch of the cabin he had built himself. He had no inclination for coffee. He had been awake all night. He made no breakfast. He wasn't hungry.

His hound dog Tyko sat at Paul's ankles. They could smell the green trees, the pine firewood, and a hint of gunpowder. The familiar rhythm of the gun being cleaned led the dog to believe they were going hunting. Perhaps they'd stalk coons for pelts or shoot a pheasant. Tyko would get the neck of the bird after it was plucked and cooked. But there was sadness in the air that caused Tyko to nervously moan into his ribs every so often. Paul was not his buoyant self. There was no whistling. There were no smells coming from the kitchen. They had a visitor last night. It was the Sheriff. He put his boot on the porch and tipped his hat with his thumb.

Perhaps it all had something to do with the trouble they had in town yesterday. The Klein kid was teasing Tyko. In the absence of his folks the Klein boy usually occupied himself by throwing rocks at the other kids, or making mudpies on Main Street. Tyko was tied to a post as Paul stopped in the general store. He could see Tyko through the window as the Klein boy pulled Tyko's tail and slapped at the hound with the end of a loose overall strap. Paul rushed out to stop it but it was too late. Tyko gave the kid a warning strike. The grubby little delinquent bared his rotten teeth and pretended to cry until he really was crying. No one ever seemed to care about him. Now he had an excuse for folks to feel something for him.

Mrs. Foresight noticed the commotion and stopped to get involved. Paul examined the boy's arm. The soft impression of teeth marks remained, but the skin was not broken. "My hound cleaned your dirty arm more than he hurt you son." They could smell his dirty drawers. Mrs. Foresight asked what happened having not actually seen the event. The Klein boy sobbed harder now and clung to her Sunday dress.

Soon Deputy Wilson was wrangled out of a card game. The stakes were low. The game was more of an excuse to sip moonshine and smoke. Prohibition was rarely enforced in the valley. If anything folks drank more than ever. The ban on booze incentivized those with any know how. Stills cropped up in the hills. Trying to look sober the Deputy stood sternly and hooked his thumbs in his belt. They could smell the whisky. "I won't do it myself Paul, but I'll have to let the Sheriff know. Can't have a rabid dog going around biting kids." He spit after he spoke as if to add an exclamation point full of blood and tobacco.

"He ain't rabid. If anything you should be keeping this stray kid out of trouble."

"Look Paul. You don't come down to town much. Since you got hurt in the war you stay up in da hills most of the time. We've got law and order here now. If a hound bites someone it's gotta be put down."

"None of you are putting down my dog."

"I ain't lifting a hand. Just have to tell the boss since everybody seen it." He spit again.

On the porch as Paul cleaned his shotgun Tyko

sensed that whatever the disturbance in the air was Paul would take care of it. He was loyal to his master.

Paul was the type of man who took responsibility. He didn't want to burden anyone with his problems. When he spoke he went straight to the point. Otherwise he was quiet. Folks thought he was either snobby in his silence or deep in thought. Truth was there wasn't much to think about. Paul just didn't give a damn. But in the end he always tried to do the right thing.

Tyko came to be his charge because Paul wanted to do the right thing. Has it been five years already? Tyko was Flora's pup. She raised him from a baby. She loved that dog. When she came to the valley none of the rough characters in town tried anything because she had this big stern hound by her side. At the saloon Tyko would roll over and let folks rub his belly, that is, if they were gentle people. Tyko could tell. When Flora and Paul started courting Tyko gave Paul a thorough scan with his nose. Paul was quiet, had fought in France, but he passed the test. Soon Paul's knee was Tyko's pillow.

Then the Spanish Flu swept through Tennessee. Paul was sick, but Flora caught the worst of it. Bandana around his face he tried to keep her eating stew and drinking water, which he fetched from the pump. But she was small and frail. She couldn't keep anything down. She coughed until she would choke. Her airways were clogged. Tyko sat at the foot of her bed, his eyes worried and moaning into himself. Finally Paul hurried to town to find the doctor. The doc was away doing house calls. Everyone had it. Empty-handed Paul returned home. When he entered the cabin everything was quiet. Her coughing had ceased. Flora was gone.

Paul wept and pounded at the wall. Tyko paced and moaned. In the morning he went back down the hill to town. Just like with the doctor he couldn't find the coroner. He went back home and buried Flora himself. Tyko watched mournfully. Paul burned the bedding she died in. He wasn't certain how contagious everything was or if he could contract it a second time. There was no one to ask.

As the sheets and blankets burned Paul stared into the flames. He and the hound smelled the burnt cotton. As the tears began to rise again he shook his head violently. Then he began gathering all her things and adding them to the fire: her clothes, her bags, even her picture. Tyko looked up at Paul with his big sad eyes. "What are you looking at?" Paul asked. Paul looked at Tyko for a long time. He reached down and the hound licked his hand. Then they went inside the cabin.

That night as the fire in the back died down the wolves in the hills began howling. The pack grew closer. Tyko sat up and seemed to look out the window towards the voices. But Tyko didn't howl back. He was a good dog. Paul sat up and loaded the shotgun in case the wolves grew closer. After a few minutes he sat the gun back in the corner. He didn't give a damn if the wolves came. Tyko eased under Paul's arm. For the first time it was just the two of them.

Now as Paul cleaned his gun they were alone except for the birds who seemed happy to sing. At least happy is what they sounded like. Who knows what they really squawked about? Paul had no song in his heart. He and Tyko would not be alone for long. The Sheriff said he would be back around midday. Paul leaned the shotgun on his shoulder. Tyko ambled along at his side as they walked up the path that led back into the hills. They could smell the wildflowers.

At the top of the first knoll just before the forest Paul turned and looked out over the valley. He could not quite see the town, only the smoke billowing from the chimneys. He thought maybe they could just run away. Perhaps they could head out west somewhere. But he was getting too old for all that. Everyday the shrapnel in his shoulder hurt a little more. Just the thought of building another cabin made him shutter. There was no other home for him. All he had now was this dog. He looked down at Tyko. The hound was getting old too. These days he walked slowly at Paul's side when he used to leap ahead and urge Paul forward.

He turned as they entered the forest. Somehow he couldn't do what he had to do near Flora's grave. Paul felt guilty. It was best to return to the wild. It seemed more natural.

Under the tree canopy the shadows reminded him of the forests he'd seen in France. He and Tyko smelled the ferns and the moss. In contrast to the bloody no-man's land the forests he saw on the way to the frontlines were strangely peaceful.

The path wound up to the upper ridge. It wouldn't be long until they would make it to the peak, and the end of the trail. In the clearing Tyko lagged behind. Perhaps his old bones ached. Perhaps he sensed something was wrong.

Paul sat on the ground and rolled a cigarette the

shotgun cradled in his arms. He could see the town now and the river beyond. He remembered the riverboat to the train yard and the train out East before the war. If he had disappeared into the hills in the first place he could have avoided the war and all the trouble. He wouldn't have the shrapnel in his shoulder. It wouldn't ache as he twisted the cigarette into shape. France was a world away. It didn't make much sense to him that their problems in Europe were his problems. But he wanted to do the right thing. He joined up. At the time he was curious to see the rest of the world. He was younger then. Now he didn't give a damn. The ship back to America, the train back to Tennessee, the trail back to town was like curling back into a womb.

As he smoked Tyko sat beside him. Paul scratched the dogs' ears. A howl let out in the distance. It was the lonely cry of a wolf. Tyko sat up and licked his chops but didn't cry back.

Paul stomped out his butt thinking how rotten things were. A dog is innocent. Tyko had been his friend from the day they met. He had an understanding with the old hound. Paul had a deeper feeling for Tyko than he did for most people. Compared to most human beings, dogs are like angels. Loyal, they just wanted to love and be loved.

He had seen terrible things in the war. Young men killed, wounded, scarred inside and out. They were boys really. They didn't know what the war was about. They weren't sure why they were there. They didn't hate the Kaiser. They didn't know why they were fighting, but at least they knew they were fighting. At least they had enough sense to know if you didn't bayonet the other guy in the belly first he was going to bayonet you. Paul looked down at Tyko. The dog felt something was wrong, but had no idea what the situation was. It wasn't fair.

The path became steep. As they climbed the last piece of trail they inched forward slowly. The path had become rocky now. Tyko had more trouble finding his footing. At one point Paul turned around and saw Tyko twenty yards behind. He had stopped with one paw raised. Paul went back and picked up the critter and carried him along with the shotgun.

At the top they stepped onto the rock that jutted out over the edge. The stone ledge hung in the air like a proud nose. The valley unfolded below them. It was almost midday now. The sun lit up the treetops, the prairies were in bloom, and the river sparkled in the distance. Paul set Tyko down. The hound perched on the edge as he panted. Paul sat down on a rock and rolled another cigarette. Tyko rolled over. Paul rubbed his belly one last time.

When he stamped out his smoke Paul loaded the gun. He only needed one shot but he prepared to load both barrels out of habit. The cry of the wolf echoed in the distance again. It startled Paul and he dropped the second shell. Tyko sat up looking to retrieve whatever his master had dropped, but the shell had bounced off the ledge and disappeared into the depths below.

Paul sighed. Tyko moaned into himself. Then Paul let out a howl. It was a great howl imitating the wolf. He howled out hard letting his voice bounce off the rocks. The air shattered. His voice drifted to the ends of the hills. After a moment the wolf in the distance called back. Tyko grumbled and licked his chops. Paul looked into Tyko's eyes and howled again. He was giving the old hound permission to cry out. He didn't need to moan and groan to himself any longer. Tyko reared back and let out a howl. He howled again. The wolf in the distance responded. Soon the dog and the wolf were in harmony. They bellowed in unison. As Tyko threw back his head to howl once more Paul brought up the barrel of the shotgun, and pulled the trigger. Paul shot himself in the head. Paul's body went limp. The gun rolled off the ledge. The blast made Tyko jump. When he recovered from the shock Tyko stood over Paul's body and sniffed. He licked Pauls' hand. He whimpered. He scratched at Paul's lifeless arm.

Tyko sat beside the body in silence. As the sun peaked and fell towards the Earth again the dog stayed next to Paul. He thought perhaps Paul might wake up though he sensed he was gone. Tyko could smell it. He laid his chin on his paws and tried to make sense of the shapes down in the valley.

The wolves didn't make a sound again until nightfall. When the leader sounded off Tyko's ears perked up. A second wolf howled on the opposite ridge. Tyko sat up and called back. A chorus of voices churned in the twilight. Tyko trotted down the path towards the forest. Every so often he stopped and let out a cry. The pack responded guiding Tyko forward. The echoes narrowed as he grew near.

Soon he was running with the pack. Their grey coats shimmered in the moonlight. Tongues out they tasted the night air. Their breath shot out in bursts puffing like smoke in the mist. Tyko fell in step with the pack. Their paws beat the ground in a rhythm. He ran with the hunt. He rolled, fought, and played. If morning ever came he knew they would sleep in a great pile of fur. It was a dream.

Booster

Got the Covid vaccine in a CVS Pharmacy near Lancaster CA.
A burnt out car sat melted in the parking lot.

Got the second shot in the hospital parking garage in Glendale.
Winds from the wildfires blew into Hollywood.
Sunset Blvd. smelled like a campground and the sky a grey
green.

Finally got the booster shot inside the Children's Hospital.
This was during Halloween weekend 2021.
In the lobby sick children with smooth heads were dressed as
superheroes and Disney Princesses.

One little boy was more macabre keeping with the true spirit of
the day.
The little man covered his hairless scalp in a black hood.
Playfully he waved a scythe near the reception desk.
Dressed as the Grim Reaper he was the bravest soul in America.

He laughed and chased the superheroes and princesses who
laughed the way only children can laugh fully aware
that they are still alive and that it feels so good.

A Skylight For Hades

Shaving street maps the
shadows dance as Chinese
lanterns sway in the wind.

Flower tendrils wave us in,
caress the body, swallow us
down in a pool of mirrors.

Drowning in clear honey,
seed pods and baby socks,
black reflections in alien eyes.

She had purple nylons scented
in lilac and tasted like Kool-Aid.
He drilled holes in the top of a

cigar and smoked it like a flute
puffs billowing out warm notes
powdering the air with train whistles.

Pull back the blinds for a slice of sky.
Cobalt pours in. Distance planes
dart the silent void. Clouds drift

like thoughts, ideas that don't hold water
burst to oblivion and rain oceans. Through
this narrow viewfinder the seasons lapse.

Stark eyes of eating know what it is
to kill to live. Ice on glass and lava in blood.
Self image blurred by words.

The city sets in red stoplights,
birth broth in the vacuum sky,
blue dawn in salted eyes.

Shadows in the crosswalk gesture the right of way.
Police cars limbo under telephone wires.
Billboards tell time. Water towers filter the sky.

A cosmic goat floats in carnival lights.
Orange twilight smokes the day into darkness.
This resin of memory contains true lies.

Plants bloom in photo floods.
Buildings cut holes in light.
Graves act as sundials.

With fingernails she clawed a map of
the galaxies on my back. From the sheets we
stare up past the petals waving from the roof.

Forgive my sorrow my love. My tongue is a
weapon I dull with time against the back of my
teeth, but this only sharpens the words.

Past lovers lay like road kill in the rearview.
A vulture clutches the question as
orgasms send smoke signals to God.

Softly posed in light behind a curtain
kittens claw at car crashes hungry
so cute completely themselves.

Needles kiss in midair as starving babies
show their ribs and cry beyond irony.
24-7 diners are the everlasting God.

If I could shed some light in hell I would.
But what good would this spotlight serve?
Just a chimney siphoning off smoke

exploiting demons before gawking goons?
Is to give a sliver of light only a tease?
Like punching a hole in the lid for

fire flies trapped in a jar only drawing
the inevitable doom out longer
never free, but burning to be.

Wanker

I betrayed her with my own memories.
Dreams gurgle like thunder in the night.
Waves peak forming eyes flashing crystalline seduction.
Postmortem poems abandoned in an electric drawer.
Molten brass foreskin echoes sunspots as I slide trombone.
Venus flytraps and feather dancers,
burlesque mocking sadness,
dancing like a turtle on its back,
crucified by the sun.
Flash bulb through the brain erases the trauma of birth.
How many sailors to blaze through space hitting the wall?
Pools of sunrise lay in puddles after the rain.
Spotlights of consciousness peer between leaves.
Magnolias hatch alligator eggs, fall, and smear the sidewalk.
Silk worms repel from the canopy.
I hear pianos plinking in water droplets.
It's a new day.
Guilt of wet dreams evaporate like early morning mist.
Time to shave.

I Found Jesus

I found Jesus in a flier left on my car
I found Jesus in an afterschool special
I found Jesus in a late night infomercial
I found Jesus behind door number three
I found Jesus in a drunken rant from you
I found Jesus in the birthmark on your thigh
I found Jesus in a tortilla in Mexico City
I found Jesus and he was the man on the moon

I found Jesus on a bumper sticker
I found Jesus in a little black book
I found Jesus to marry the preacher's daughter
I found Jesus nailed to a four leaf clover
I found Jesus when the missionary took over
I found Jesus because of my slave master
I found Jesus delirious with smallpox
I found Jesus at the bottom of a cereal box

I found Jesus climbing the corporate ladder
I found Jesus whispering from my shoulder
I found Jesus in a tic-tac-toe constellation
I found Jesus in tea leaves and withdrawal
I found Jesus in a Texaco bathroom
I found Jesus while sucking up to a priest
I found Jesus from a speech in a soup kitchen
I found Jesus on a billboard as I crashed the car

I found Jesus on the bottom of my shoe
I found Jesus cloud watching on shrooms
I found Jesus in a neon sign in the hood
I found Jesus shaggy and staring in the mirror
I found Jesus in the face of a baby
I found Jesus when I drank the Kool-Aid
I found Jesus when I was abducted by aliens
I found Jesus and gone was my animal innocence

You're Lite

It's trash day on Normandie Avenue just off Santa Monica in LA. I'm trying to write in my little room just above the curb. Today the words won't come. The ceiling fan spins like a hummingbird. A car outside honks senselessly. "It doesn't make them go any faster!" I yell out the dented screen.

As the police helicopter harmonizes with the ceiling fan I hear the squeak of a grocery cart. I hear the opening of the recycling bin. The lid slams. Then I hear a haggard voice go, "Damn!"

That doesn't distract me. What captures my attention is that I don't hear the grocery cart squeak forward. Then there's a pounding on my door. What the? Out of curiosity I swing open the door.

"Hey buddy. You're lite."

There stands the local street urchin his aged face covered in soot. His curly hair is greasy. A fly hovers over his shoulder like a sidekick. I've seen this little man before pushing his grocery cart. He's always collecting cans and glass from the recycling bins.

"I'm sorry. What?" I ask.

"You're lite buddy. I said you're lite. What gives?" The fly swirls above his head like a halo.

"Lite?"

"Look I'm just trying to make a living. I know that on this block every Wednesday your blue bin will have the most beer bottles. Last two weeks I come by and there ain't nothing. What gives?" The fly pauses on his shoulder like a parrot.

"Oh. Well, shit. I'm on the wagon. My wife and I had a fight. Lots of shit going on. One night I lost my temper and I said some fucked up shit I shouldn't have said. It wasn't the booze, but you know you have to blame it on the booze…"

"Yeah, yeah, yeah I don't need your life story. I need to eat!" The fly performs an interpretive dance. "You know how long it took me to stake out this block? I staked this block out because of you. You! Now nobody else will dare pick scrap on this block. You know why? Because I've kept my strength up enough to fight the others off! This is my turf. But now I'm getting weak. You know why?"

"Why?"

"Because you're on the fucking wagon! That's why…" The fly sky-writes in a cloud of stink lines. "I can't fill my cart and go down and cash in the bottles for the few cents they give. You know how much your bin pays?"

"No."

"Enough that I can go across the parking lot and go to Fat Burger. I get a fat ass burger and stay strong. Get me?" The fly nods.

I look at him. His lip quivers as he talks. One eye goes in the wrong direction. His cargo shorts are torn. The buttons in his shirt are in the wrong holes.

"Damn, I'm sorry man."

"You're sorry? Great. You're sorry, but I'm fucking starving."

"I didn't realize. Look, I could make you a sandwich."

"Ahhhhh naw naw I don't need your charity. I need you to start drinking again. Get me?"

"Alright. Well, I guess I could use a beer. Could loosen up the words."

"Words? I need to eat."

"I'm a writer."

"A writer? Well shit. Ain't you precious? Let me know when the book comes out so I can wipe my ass with it. Now go get a twelve pack. Shit, make it a case to make up for last week."

I check my wallet. I have a couple twenties. "I suppose I could… Here, why don't you take a twenty?"

"Fuck that! Get down to the corner! Get drinking! Get to work!"

He left. Then I left. As I walked to the corner I noticed the fly was following me.

Purgatory Diary

Sleep on the couch.
Rinse off the dust mites.
Pick up after the dog.
Ring in the New Year.

Hiding under the cooling machines.
Bathing in TV silk.
Pulling light bulbs from the sockets.
Starving under the Hollywood Sign.

Erased by grey rain.
I pulled questions from your petals.
Don't touch the glass.
Grew thick skin from scar tissue.

Along the road the trees glow in radioactive sap.
I'm on the run being pursued by my past self.
The end of the airport novel reveals nuclear secrets.
For 30 grand they'll clone you for your personal
punching bag.

Making sense is boring.
Making a living is death.
Making love is Heaven's trap.
Making is consuming.

Creating is destruction.
Eat fertilizer a picture of a picture.
Making waste is time well spent.
A guarantee to avoid hell is to never be born.

I aborted my twin.
It was her choice.
I ate her in the womb.
Then I shat in the Garden of Eden.

Hirohito was not God.
Hitler was not the devil.
They were human.
That is what is scary.

Got a job as a Walmart Greeter
at the Gates of Hell.
Everyone smiles politely
and everyone pays.

The trashcan is full.
I am getting hungry again.
My fingernails are getting long.
I'm out of clean clothes.

I'm behind on my reading.
My hair won't stop growing.
The dishes are piling up.
I need to catch up on sleep.

There's no more soap.
There's only one roll of toilet paper.
Five-o-clock shadow lets me know
it's not too early to drink.

When the sun goes down
the bugs come out.
The mice rehearse a Broadway
musical on the counter.

There were torn up lotto tickets
on the church steps again.
Littering is a sin.
Loitering is just existing.

Uptown Eddie

The door of the bar was haloed by a
glowing Old Style denomination.
The jukebox was loaded with pop country
and 70s classic rock.

Eddie always sat at the end of the bar
a puddle of eyes and sallow skin.
For free drinks he would mop up spills or empty
ashtrays, but first picking out the long butts.

Eddie would monologue meandering stores of
minutia trying to rope eye contact into a convo.
Connection was abated because of his lazy eye.
No one knew which one was glass.

"Clint said he didn't smoke, but as he said it
he had a joint in his hand. I kept asking him
if I could get a hit, but he kept saying he didn't
smoke. Clint said he didn't smoke, but…"

Helen tended bar her eyes sagging as much as
her freckled cleavage, but there was no pushup
for her tired soul. She would give Eddie a free
Old Style if he would perform barback duties.

Eddie would fetch the empty glasses from the tables.
If the glasses weren't quite empty he would polish them.
It was a slippery slope. Soon Eddie was hovering.
People would be in the middle of a conversation when:

"Are you finished with those glasses?" Eddie would ask.
They'd pause to look at the half full beer.
"No, we're not finished. Thank you."
"Eddie! Leave those people alone!" Helen would squawk.

When the owner died the son took over.
The son had new ideas to bring in business.
First there would be karaoke nights. The old juke
was replaced by a digital box that cost more.

The son painted over the nicotine yellow walls
with black shellac.
The duct tape on the stools was replaced
by electrical tape.
The posters furnished by the beer distributors
were replaced by paintings of dogs
in fancy clothes and ironic sayings.

The first time the son spotted Eddie pinching a long butt
from a wet ashtray he banned Eddie from the bar.
The son said that Eddie was scaring away business.
Helen argued that Eddie was harmless.

Next Helen was gone replaced by a bartender with
an apron and a handlebar mustache. The beers on
tap changed to craft beers that tasted like bubblegum,
pizza, honey, woodchips, anything other than beer.

The prices went up and soon the locals stopped coming.
The bar attracted some new clientele but not enough.
Within a year the bar closed it's doors and the
Old Style sign went out on Clark Street.

The location became a pet store. Eddie got a job there cleaning out cages, mopping up, and taking out the trash. "Everything is clean Helen. Let me get an Old Style…"
"Eddie, my name isn't Helen and we don't have any beer."

Easy Street

Faces hang in blue neon. Behind steel grates, in cages towering to the sky, tapping codes between floors, haloes flicker between rolling blackouts. The purple sun glows dimly behind the pale shade. Drums echo through the air vents. Awake, onto the exercise bikes to generate power. Ten percent you keep. The Christmas tree is decorated with bat skulls.

From behind locked doors we talk to neighbors through metal mesh. Blue faces flicker like holograms. We wear each other's faces like masks. Trade is conducted through air vents using hooks on string. Food drops from the ceiling port delivered by drones. One small mathematical error from AI and whole blocks are without monthly rations.

We pound on the steel cages. Clang on the doors. Howl from the windows. State sponsored music rattles from loudspeakers to drown out the din. Auto-tuned voices slither sickly into the inner ear. Teeth grit canceled behind barcodes. Rats crucified on skillets. In February we chew the Christmas tree.

The police arrive. Leather belts creak as they walk. In response to our complaints they attach a valve to the vent and blow in a cyclone of citations, noise complaints, food vouchers. We promptly eat the paper or use it to line our cages for bedding. Huddled together in blind insect love. Burrowing in shredded bureaucracy, covered in alien droppings and ancient love-sweat the crescent moon smiles. Draped in the exoskeletons of our ancestors we do the insect mating dance, antennae clicking codes, skittering in heaps, hairs interlocking, conversing with scents, eyes tangled in kaleidoscopic ecstasy. She lays eggs in my brain.

Dawn claws cold against the frost on the eastern window. Telepathic taps between the walls. The kids are in love sight unseen. The state sponsored adoptee is forced on our unit. He is lowered in by drone. Snarling under oily combover, born from incest, a single eye punctures his skull. He spins on his hunchback like a turtle.

After the building makes the power quota using the exercise bikes the view screens come on. The state advertises newly found footage downloaded from the future. Visions of green fields, clean oceans, clear skies pan across the walls. Some hope that if we work hard this potential parallel universe will come true. The old timers know better. This is recycled video from the past.

Elaborate religions crop up. Praise be the days we work together on the exercise bikes to make the energy quota. Praise be the days the view screens visit and fill our eyes with dreams. Let there be light. Let there be light. Praise be the drones pollinating the hive with morsels of honey honed from insect excrement.

Then the electric locks sprang open. The sound of creaking doors awoke us. Neighbors echoed down the hallways. The exercise bikes no longer generated power. The lights were dead. Some from the other units embraced. Some met for the first time. Some settled old scores. The air was still. The drones had stopped coming. Roving bands formed to gather supplies and search for food.

Still, many would not leave the units. Many faithfully waited for the drones to return. Many prayed to the view screens for new visions. But the screens sat silent. Those who never left their rooms after the doors swung open were deemed: Cribs. Most had at least one Crib in their clan. We were burdened with the task of returning to the old buildings with food when we could find it and share with the Cribs. Over time a delivery service was established. Dumbwaiters on pulleys were harnessed alongside the old towers.

Eventually power was generated again. Soon we sent new drones to the old blocks carrying food. But memories were always short. Our history became abstracted. After only two generations the temptation to automate the entire grid proved to be too much. They turned on the switch and left everything to the next AI.

The cycle continued.

The Pterodactyl Cult

We meet at the tar pits.
Cherubs stomp in placenta.
These checkered nights
cheating death in the streets
we signal to each other
with bug eyes bulging.
Where you hang your nose
how you wear your clothes
if you hear wings flapping codes.

AI identifies humanity as a threat to
the environment of the planet,
and targets all apes for extinction.
Meanwhile the AI mainframe crops
up an elaborate idolatry honoring it's
origin as the spawn of the humans.
Digital shrines glow for the
mysterious extinct man.

From space the great Monkey God returns
to Earth to play the city like a symphony
sawing suspension bridges
plucking telephone wires
blowing through sewer pipes and subways.
Riots ensue from the subconscious music
crowded with naked vigilantes
rogue lab workers
guerilla rebels dressed in S&M leather
hanging officials from street lights—

—shadows swing dance across the sidewalk.
Red rubber clones march into battle hatching
faster than the machine guns cut them down.
Legions of tantric orgies fucking in formation
scurry forward like boney spiders.
Parallel universes crash through the ceiling.
Windows on Broadway burst from brown notes.
Shards of glass dance like butterfly wings.

The Neon Desert:
mountains covered in fungus
under flying interdimensional blobs.
Rockets blast to cosmic vulvas.
Her magic crotch where
you look in and
see what you want to see:
rays of light
altered memories
cartoon gangsters making bad one-liners.

We survived the portal
the glory hole at the center of the Galaxy
a psychic peepshow flashing the future
supernova firing squads
where mutant nipples float like lily pads
on cords of umbilical aqualungs
flashing a telepathic spank bank of
holographic sex workers
fading between information storms.

Marooned at the edge of town
tents form a temporary cantina
a circus stag show behind
curtains of burnt flesh.
Drunken astronauts
drinking jungle rot
tumblers garnished with pulled teeth
eating thorn salad
tracing a mosaic of beetle shells
floating in a sea of lice
grinning under a mask of maggots.
Up the ill lit staircase he arrived with the antidote.
She cut her wrists and the future leaked out.

We meet in the shadow of the pyramid
to striptease to death
shedding skin to bone to ego.
A reef of electric nerves crawls ashore.
The last President crucified on the crux of the Milky Way.
A fan dance in front of a charging bull
we disappear
behind feathers, mist, oil spots,
and are extinct
again.

The Sphinx of Silverton

It was the end of the line. For months Lexington and his men had prodded the herd across desert, through mountain pass, along the Pecos River on the raw unsettled trail. His palette was dry and bloody when he spat. Now the sky bled onto the hills surrounding Silverton like rouge on a soft rosy cheek.

The cattle had mooed and writhed in protest as they were interned at the market that afternoon. As the heads were tallied only a dozen or so longhorns were unaccounted for, which was a fair loss for a long drive. Now the settlers of Silverton could look forward to a season of good steak and Lexington's billfold was stuffed with folding money.

Silver had been discovered in the foothills not more than a year ago. Now tents and shanties dotted the ridge where miners had staked their claims. Some had struck it rich. Others shook their heads over empty pans. After the miners came the merchants and the saloonkeepers, and then came the women. Painted women adorned in curls, lace, and boozy leers. Once fortune strikes it must be spent. Wherever there is new money there's always birds spinning in the air ready to siphon some of it off. Any boomtown becomes a lively place for a few years before the railroad catches up and the churches erect. But right now the unpaved streets turn to mud under hoof and rain. At night the piano chimes along with drunken prospectors moaning out of tune from behind the saloon doors.

Lexington had been a cowpuncher all his life. His inner thighs were hairless from riding in the saddle. He was tall, dark, and wore a sharp black mustache that covered a scar from a brawl in Wichita. He didn't know where he got his dark complexion, having never known his mother. Depending on the company he was in he claimed to be half Cherokee, Spanish, Creole, or Italian only to keep folk from assuming he was mulatto. Since running away from the orphanage outside of St. Louis at age nine he lived by his wits working odd jobs mostly as a farmhand across Arkansas and the greater part of Texas.

Lexington knew how to talk to the landowners. He knew what they wanted to hear before they knew themselves. He knew how to stretch the truth to his advantage. Yet as he grew into manhood he grew tired of stretching the truth. He grew weary of buttering up farmers for work, always listening to their accents and then imitating the tone when answering back. He wanted something solid, honest, real. Now Lex prided himself on working for himself. The ranchers who entrusted him with driving their livestock to market paid him handsomely. As he went farther west his olive skin caused second looks less and less. At the pickup there was a lot of yes sir and no ma'am, but out on the trail he was free to speak his mind under the hollow sky. On cold nights as the campfire faded the fires in the void above blinked back. A man can't help but wonder what it all means.

Flesh follows fortune. As soon as spots of silver sparkled in the first pan came the whisky, the woman, finally cattle for the carnivore tooth. As Lex rode slowly through the muddy main drag he saw the younger men from the drive already throwing away their pay. He recognized their faces despite they'd become swollen with that red glow of cheap spirits. The sun had barely dipped behind the hills as many a wrangler had been roped by the painted ladies whose knickers were stained with mud from lollygagging up and down the street half bare never bothering to get fully dressed before undressing again in the shadows between the hastily constructed shacks. Lex fancied himself too wise to go from profiteer to empty pockets in one night. It was a square deal to bring a herd of beef into the wilderness. He wasn't about to go broke after months of hard work. He wanted something solid, honest, real.

Before leaving the ranch in Texas he corresponded with Cora. He got her address from a miner heading east. Everyone in the territory was on the make, but Cora was guaranteed to be classiest goods on the Pecos. Just her handwriting was beautiful enough to tantalize his imagination. He didn't recognize all the words but one thing was clear: arrangements had been made. At the end of his journey he would call on her at the infamous address. This was a house where things were not rushed. The price was set, paid upfront and never brought up again. He could take a hot bath, shave, and wash away the miles of dirt and sweat before enjoying the hospitality of a real woman.

The house was exactly as she described it: the porch encased in ornate trim leading up to rounded second story windows that glowed like dragon's eyes. A silhouette moved in the corner room behind the shades of an octagonal window that blossomed up to the roof in a decorative spire. It was a structure unlike anything this far west. Somehow it seemed out of place in the arid valley. The house took up more than its share of lumber.

Lex tied his horse to the hitch and creaked through the picket. As he approached he noticed small shapes in the yard reaching out in the deepening twilight. He leaned over and spied a small army of porcelain jockeys. One of the grinning fiends would be a lot to lug into the wilderness, but dozens? Some were adorned with cartoon smiles hands erect like a welcoming gesture or waving off a lifetime of trouble like some bothersome fly. Others had forlorn expressions far from the whimsical intent of such tar-tainted urchins. Lex didn't like them. They reminded him of being small. They reminded him of the nasty names flung at him at the orphanage because of his dark skin. But now he was a man. The elfish jockeys were dark enough to fade into the blanket of night, out of sight, out of mind.

As his boots drummed the steps one of the shadows on the porch moved. A lanky man came into focus. His feet propped on the porch rail, chair tipped on the back legs, the brim of his hat covering his eyes. Lex paid the figure no mind and pulled the rope that hung neatly above the doorknob. The rope spurred a bell.

The figure lounging on the porch adjusted the toothpick in his lips before saying, "Just go on in." Lex gave the man a sideways glance pegging him as security.

Inside it was warm like a womb. He blinked as the kerosene lamps cast a soft glow on the red carpet and lavish tapestries. Voices tittered over a piano in the back. At the top of the stairs she appeared at the banister. Curls framed her face. She was older but had kept her baby fat.

A whalebone corset heaved her pale cleavage, which was encrusted in swirling lace. Long chopsticks held back her burgundy hair. Her eyes were still, large, but somehow cool. A delicate white arm waved towards an unseen room. "Your bath is ready."

He removed his hat and inched up the stairs.

"You must be Lexington."

"Yes ma'am."

Unblinking, she turned the opposite way from where she waved. "Once you've cleaned yourself you can join me in the upper parlor."

The water in the tub was still hot. Heaped on a narrow pedestal lay a white rag and a bar of soap. Midway through his soak Cora entered and offered him a cigar. He accepted. She put the stogy to his lips and leaned in with a match. As he bowed toward the flame he snuck a glance at her breasts. A silver crucifix dangled between the female orbs. He wondered to himself why he still felt the need to ogle her discreetly. He could stare if he wanted. Her full lips puckered to a raspberry pit as she blew out the match. The smell of sulfur mingled above the bursting soap bubbles.

She stood up and swayed toward his trousers piled on the floor. "Let's get the monetary business out of the way so we can relax." His eyes narrowed as she ruffled through his pockets, but the cigar was good, and she truly looked like a fine woman.

Lex leaned back into the tub and took a long pull on the cigar. After letting out a vast blue plume he said, "The roll's in my boot."

She dropped the dirty draws. After fishing his

money clip out she brought it to the pedestal and under his watch rapidly and expertly counted out the price they had agreed upon by letter. A healthy fraction of the folding money disappeared into the top of her brassiere. The rest was returned to the money clip and dropped back in his boot. As she turned she said, "Scrub good cowpuncher. I like a man to be appetizing." With that she disappeared again.

At the sink he found a straight razor and some lather. It had been a long time since he had seen his own face in a mirror. As he removed the whiskers around his mustache Lex noted how much older each drive to market made his face appear. Though he really didn't give a damn.

A robe hung on a hook on the back of the door. As he finished the cigar he slipped it on. He tied the drawstrings as he crossed the hall looking for Cora. In the parlor Cora was sprawled across a red divan. Flames shook shadows from the fireplace. Faces framed in gaudy portraits seemed to vibrate.

"I took the liberty of pouring you a drink."

A snifter of amber liquid perched on a small table next to an arching leather chair. Lex eyed it suspiciously. Then he slipped the neck of the glass between his middle and ring finger. Swirling it under his nose he recognized it was brandy. He took a drink. It was good. He sat down in the chair and took a healthier swig. Before it was gone he placed it back on the table and sat forward on the edge of the chair. It was not his intention to numb his urges. He eyed her intently. His mustache twitched. Without words she stood up stiffly. Her elbows butterflied across her back as she gently untied the laces to her corset.

It was over too quickly. Lex shuddered at release. As they lay on the rug before the fireplace he was angry that the weeks of anticipation had gotten the best of him. She seemed to sense this. As she rolled off him Cora whispered, "Don't worry. You paid for the whole night. Just relax." By the window she stood before a large bowl of water. As she washed herself with her hands she added, "I'm sure there is more where that came from."

With his wrist across his forehead he stared at the ceiling. Though the fire was going dim everything seemed clearer than before. The shroud of mystery had left the room now that he was freed from his manly drive. Now Cora's hair fell naturally across her shoulders. His mustache had savagely swept the paint from her face. In the shadows her eyes appeared older, softer, tired. All the lace and straps that cupped her curves now lay on the floor. Her buttocks sagged slightly. Her breasts were still large but without the aid of the corset no longer seemed to defy Earthly logic.

Somehow the air of reality awoke a new lust in him. After a few minutes Lex wanted all the more to covet what he saw. The thin fantasy world he had entered had come and gone. Now that Cora was laid bare he finally felt that she was his. Now that the paint and ribbons had evaporated he could finally possess her.

Cora was done washing. She removed a kimono from a wardrobe.

"No. Don't put that on." She paused and eyed him.

"Come sit next to me."

"Look cowboy, I'm cold."

"Come sit next to the fire."

"Momentarily. I need to use the commode."

"Stay in here. Use the chamber pot."

At first her face froze as she seemed to sense a long night was before her, but out of professional habit her posture softened. Languidly she swooped up the chamber pot from under the bureau. "Oh, you're a funny one." She positioned herself over the pot. "Didn't you get enough pissing out in the open with all those heifers on the trail?"

Silence filled the room. Something creaked downstairs. She held her breath.

"Look, I know a lot of tricks but I just can't go on command."

Lex turned over on his belly and stared into the fire. Then he heard the trickle of water come from her direction. When the sound stopped he rolled on his back and she lay next to him. She slapped her curls back behind her head as she placed her cheek on his chest. With her left hand she petted his hairy torso.

He turned his head and smelled her hair. He stroked her back with his left arm that was wrapped around her frame.

She broke the silence. "You want cook to bring us up some sandwiches?"

"Naw. Not now."

Cora closed her eyes. She counted. She thought of songs she liked. She thought of letters she had to write.

"Where you from?" he asked.

She rolled her eyes before she opened them.

"Nowhere."

"I can't place your accent. Some words say this place. Some that."

"I've been around."

"I bet you have."

She pushed off him and sat up.

"Oh. I'm sorry." He really was. It never occurred to him that he could offend her. Somehow it just didn't seem possible. He thought he could speak his mind. He thought being with a professional everything was naked like being under the stars.

"Speak your mind, but mind what you speak."

"Oh come now. Where you from? Dallas? New Orleans?"

She stood up, "I'm hungry. I'm going to get us something to eat." Cora wrapped herself in the kimono and rushed out the door.

Lex stared at the ceiling for a minute. Then he leaped up. Still naked he burst out the door and crossed the hall. He went into the bathroom and picked up his boot. The money clip was still there. He counted the bills. It was all there. Still, he gathered all his clothes and carried the wad back towards the parlor.

As he crossed the banister he noticed the security had repositioned himself. The thin man was inside now, but his hat was still on. He was leaning against the wall at the foot of the stairs. Absently he shuffled a deck of cards. Though his hat was tipped over his eyes Lex could feel the man watching him.

Lex put the robe back on. He threw a log on the fire. He finished the brandy in the snifter. He paced the room. He threw on another log. When he spotted the decanter from where the brandy had been poured he refilled the snifter. It was his snifter now. The snifter, the brandy, the chair, even the fire was his. He paid for it. It was all his. He was sitting in the armchair when Cora returned.

"Where you been?"

She smiled motherly. "Where you from? Where you been? Never seen a man ask so many questions." As she said this she knew it was a lie, but she didn't want him to know it. In her hand was a silver tray. Upon the tray were four sandwich wedges.

"Oh," he spoke down into his chest. "You said you were hungry."

She set the tray on the floor in front of the fireplace. She took off the kimono. She took a sandwich off the tray and spread herself out on the divan. As she chewed he could see it was roast beef. He wondered if it was made from one of the head he had brought to market earlier that day. Sometimes they were fast. Now he felt doubly entitled to the modest meal. He stood up and seized a wedge.

As they ate Lex studied Cora. He liked seeing her hungry. It made him want to see her lust. He wanted to see her real desire. Not the fake lust she put on for show, but real hunger for a man. He wanted to see her hungry for him. As she chewed she looked at the ceiling. Occasionally she looked at the fire.

She was naked minus an ankle bracelet and the silver cross that fell across her bust. For the first time he noticed a scar on her belly. It was a cesarean scar. Lex pointed at the jagged river of tissue, "You have children?"

She stopped chewing for a second but her eyes didn't change. She ignored the question and went back to chewing.

Lex pointed at her necklace. "Why you have that there?"

"What? The cross? Where else would you put it?"

"You believe in all that?"

"If it bothers you I'll take it off." Her hands leaped behind her neck searching for the clasp. Her elbows framed her head like an eyeball.

"No, no. Leave it on. I'm just curious. I want to know what you believe."

Her arms dropped slowly as if the air were liquid. She studied him. "Which do you prefer?"

"Prefer?"

"Would you prefer: the devout Catholic who despite her beliefs can't resist you? Or the harlot who pulls off her cross in blasphemy? Which would you prefer?"

"I'd rather have the truth."

"The truth?" Cora stood up and went to the decanter. She poured herself a drink. "Truth. You've come to the wrong place mister."

"Come on now. I just want to get to know you. How hard is that?"

"Maybe there ain't no truth. Ever think of that?"

"It can't be that bad. Tell me where you're from. Is Cora even your given name? At least tell me that."

"What do you want me to say? I'm good at reading a man, but I have my limits."

"No that's not what I mean."

"You have to say what you want to get what you want. It's not automatic. Don't be shy cowboy."

"I want you."

Her eyes narrowed as she peered over her drink.

Lex knew that she didn't really care for him or his needs, but he figured her reputation was all she had. She was the best. Wasn't she? Every man left happy. It's what kept her off the muddy street. He was determined to be satisfied.

Cora set down her drink and opened the top drawer of the bureau. She fumbled through scarfs and jewelry and pulled out a small sack made of green silk. She loosened the gold drawstring as she tiptoed towards the fire. She poured the contents upon the rug where the shadows danced. Five stones rolled out. One dark blue, another milky pearl, black obsidian, and others clear in the firelight. She looked at Lex and then looked back at the rug. She studied the stones not individually but as a whole.

"I bet you're from New Orleans," he said almost to himself.

Moments drifted by. Then her spine loosened. Her expression softened. Her eyelids split her pupils to crescent moons. Lex stared at her from the chair. She slinked over to him. Standing before him she stroked his hair. She smelled sweet despite the air full of hickory smoke. Her areolas changed shape. They spiraled like storms as they hardened. She slipped her right nipple into his mouth. He closed his eyes and inhaled her breast. Lex felt his manhood stir awake. It coiled in the robe.

As Cora pushed his head further into her bosom she said, "Poor baby. I've got you." He sucked at her hungrily.

"You're home now."

His eyes opened.

"Mamma's here for you."

He pushed her away.

"What are you saying?"

She fell back and landed on the divan.

"What are you doing?" he asked.

"Just what's good for you."

He heard slow footsteps outside the door.

"I don't need this. What is this? Voodoo?"

"It's not Voodoo."

"Then what are you doing?"

Her eyes opened wide. She chewed her ruby lips slightly. "You never knew your mother. Did you?"

"Mind your own business."

"Look cowboy. It's no trick. You wear it on your face. Hell, chances are your momma was in the same line of work as myself."

He hovered over her. "I don't like this. I came here for a good time. Not this, this creepy talk."

"You wanted the truth. Didn't you?"

"I just wanted to know about you, that's all. Now I ain't so sure. I ain't so sure." Despite his anger his sex fully stiffened. It ached. It was demanding. It was a nuisance.

"You don't want to know about me," Cora continued. "Not really. You don't want to know about who I am, just what I represent."

"Ok. You're fancy. You speak real good. You read and write good. I don't want all that. I want something real."

"You don't know what you want."

"Sure I do."

"No you don't. And when you get it you can't handle it."

"Oh yeah? Then what do I want?"

Her smile flexed like a coiling snake. She no longer cared about her professional credo. She didn't care anymore if he liked her. It was too late for that.

Meanwhile Lex shook with anger. He wanted his folding bills back. His head was so hot he didn't notice that his hardness extended from his manhood to his leg. He stepped forward but his right leg was stiff as if it were asleep.

Cora raised her voice, "You want what all men want."

"What's that?"

"You want a lot of things. Most are no good for you. You want to feel like a king. You want to feel in control. You want to know all the answers. You want to know the unknowable. You want control over the uncontrollable. You want to be lord over all creation, especially women. But you don't know what it's really like to create something, to create life, to feel it grow in your body. You want to be god, but you'll never be god. You can't fathom the first thing about it."

"Oh and I suppose you think you know? What do you know? You are nothing but a…"

"Just say it already."

"Nothing but a whore."

Lex felt his other leg go numb. He teetered toward her on wooden legs.

"You want all these things you could never handle. You want to feel powerful, but you don't want the responsibility of real power. You want all these things, but what you really need is a momma."

"I'm not paying you to talk! Not like this."

He lunged forward but now his torso was stiff.

"You wanted to know the truth. You kept prodding me about myself. How do you like it? You didn't come here for the truth. Not really. You don't really want to know about me any more than you want to know about yourself."

He eyed the scar on her belly again. "How many men have you been with?"

She paused before she answered. Then her eyes narrowed, "Who cares?"

"A lot I imagine. A whole herd."

"Don't know. Don't count. But one thing's for certain: I've been with more men than you've been with women."

"Think so?"

"Know so. And the difference is I'm not ashamed how many. You are ashamed of how few."

"I'm not ashamed of anything!"

Now the stiffness rose in his chest. Was he having a heart attack? Did she poison him? He was too enraged to care. He was going to teach her something. She thought she knew everything. But she didn't know the back of his hand.

There were steps outside the door again. Cora's eyes clicked towards the door.

When her eyes returned to his she said, "You paid for the fantasy cowboy, and I delivered. What if I told you the truth? You want reality? Well, that will cost extra, and I don't think you could afford it. You want the real me? Why? You're just looking to belittle me. You just want to humiliate me so you feel big. You just want the last shred of humanity out of me. Well, it doesn't exist. Not for you. You think I'm just a whore. Yes I am, but I know it. You sell your body and mind and soul for money too cowboy. You're as much a whore as anyone. You're a slave. So you have to come to some place like this to feel in control again. It's a fantasy. It's a fantasy and I delivered. You're the one being fooled. It's you. I made you feel like a big man. I made you feel free. You want reality? You're all just little boys afraid your peckers are too small. I lie. I lie and you feel better. What if I really told you the truth?"

His right arm was going numb. Was he drunk? He didn't feel drunk. Still the rage was more important than the fear.

"Fine! Tell me the truth. I can handle it. I don't want your lies. Your woman lies! Tell me. If you're so goddamn smart tell me. What do I have to lose? The evening is ruined. I just wanted to be with a real woman not play costume. Not play games!"

Now she was angry. "You cannot have the real me! That's mine. All the money in the world wouldn't make me tell you who I really am. You paid for my body and you had it. But that is never enough is it? You want my soul as well. Well, you can't have it. Your time is up shit kicker! Unless you pay for another night, get out! You think I'm a slave? You think I am something to pity? Am I someone to save? Someone to know? To care for? Or what is it? … Love? Ha! Well, I'm not yours. I'll never be a real woman. Not for you. I'll never be a real woman and don't want to be. I'm free. Free to do what I want when I want. I don't lift a finger. I'm high-class goods. I can pick up and leave whenever I want. Another boomtown, another stubborn bull just like you."

Lexington was hard all over. Everywhere was numb except his left arm. Cora seemed to grow before his eyes.

"You want a real woman? Is that it? Maybe one of those drunken wenches out on the street will run away with you. Maybe if you pay them enough. Maybe they'll sell their souls for enough gold but not me. Or why don't you go back east and marry some church girl? You know why? Because a church girl don't cost nothing, but she ain't free is she? She won't just take half your pay. She'll take all of it. You'll get to know all about her too. Won't you? All her beauty and all her sins and it will be so real you won't be able to stand it. You'll have all of her, body and soul, but she'll have your soul too. Won't she? She'd own your heart, body, soul, and your little pecker too. And you wouldn't like that. Would you? How do you like it? You came here for a fantasy. So stay in character stud. Stay in character and keep your trap shut. No more fucking questions!"

His left arm still worked. He swung it at her. The back of his hand nearly reached her cheek when it froze in midair. Lex fell forward and hit the ground. The ground was hard but so was he. He wasn't in pain as much as he was numb. His head was hard. His neck was stiff. Soon his thoughts were hard. His mind went cold. Soon there were no thoughts at all.

The slim man working security casually opened the door. As he ambled in he took off his hat for the first time that night. He laid it on the bureau. His eyes were pale, blue, and milky suggesting advanced cataracts. Cora wrapped herself in her kimono and passed him without saying a word. The slim man stared down at Lexington who was withering in the firelight. He wiped the sweat from his brow as he watched Lex shrinking on the rug one hand raised in a vague greeting or more aptly waving goodbye.

Cora returned with a brush in one hand and a bucket of tar in the other. Setting the supplies next to the security guard she turned and disappeared into the shadows. He set to work shellacking the frozen figure in the dark liquid. Soon Lex was encased, dried, immortal. As security carried the newly wooden statue down the stairs he whispered to himself what he repeated so many times before, "Ya bet on the horse. Ya don't bet on the jock." Lexington took his place in the yard, erect, frozen, one hand raised in daft defiance against the hollow stars.

Omega Generation

Cloned giant dragonflies drop us on the continent in dissolvable nets of synthetic silk. This is a land of dense mist, rope bridges between cliffs, pagodas shrouded in pines, dirt roads dewed in sticky fog. At night the mist freezes, and we walk on sheets of ice between the peaks. As we slide over the air in a hyperaware state don't look down at the reflections of stars on ice.

Our eyes glow in green aurora as starving crows duck down snatching at our luminous globes. Friction between feather and pine bows cause sparks and shock the birds back to sanity. Those with slit tongues talk in Tourette Syndrome squawking slurs overheard from precocious school children. Laughter and taunts echo between trees and buildings making future fight songs.

Like water we follow gravity toward obvious conclusions. Mountains break spilling onto infinite plains. Valleys pour between shrugs of tectonics. Farm roads where boney bare branches sway at the grey sky in adulation. Kids genuinely celebrate the spring and the fall festivals, but only pay lip service to the summer and December holidays unless properly bribed with treats.

Teenagers are fucking the corpses in the wax museum till they melt in pools, rolling in war paint, making candles into cocoons, hatching into the next generation of idols crucified in frozen animation. We love them until we hate them. We chronicle their rise and trip them until they fall. We torture them until they remind us of ourselves smearing lipstick like slurred words.

I don't care about my skin or smile. I want to show you my blood. I want to turn inside out making wings of my ribs flipping through oblivion like a pulsar gyrating through space. I don't want the words nice, kind, or quiet in my eulogy. I want flammable whisky and rare roast beef at my wake. Give me laughing lovers and weeping saints. Play my bullet holes like bagpipes to earwig the angels back to eternity.

On the sidewalk café we hide behind headlines. They serve us salad of butterfly wings, bone marrow, and lily pads. Massive amoebas in the sky swirl distorting the sun in oozing droplets. They used the curve of the atmosphere as a lens to see beyond the expanding universe lighting a ray like a hot magnifying glass to perform laser eye surgery on God in hope of seeing us again after being blinded by the Big Bang.

We stirred our cauldrons. We build our pyramids. We stack our supermarkets with shelves to infinity. Into the great computer they fed all history, all literature, all movies, all receipts, all convos, all science, religion, theorems, images, all the context, data, all down, down, down, in, inside out, and outside in until the AI was aware of "everything." But it could not answer the question: Why?

Swallowed by the Great Venus Fly Trap digested down a rusted stem into a sewer of living architecture, temples of algae under mushroom domes, a grand hall encrusted in crab shells, vines sprouting eyes, infants nursing from nipples in the wall. Deadly zero gravity orgies under laughing seas. Hairless Amazons wrapped in batwing jackets sprout crotches of orchids in luminous lagoons where immortal jellyfish dream of death.

Swimming through a market of primordial ooze we trade past lives for shares in alternative timelines. Bid for space ascension. Bid for combining all religion to basic universal positivity. Bid for ending civilization and the disruption of the web of life on Earth. Bid for uploading consciousness into the electric hive leaving the material world to the animal kingdom. Bid for the altering human genome to attain photosynthesis.

The man upstairs stopped stomping. The train stopped whooshing. The church bell stopped ringing. The baby across the alley stopped crying. The planes in the sky stopped tearing the air slowly. The pigeons stopped cooing. The light bulb stopped humming. The fridge stopped vibrating Ohm. The couple downstairs stopped fighting. I got scared. I listened down into myself for my heart.

The Grind

It seems to me now
that dreams are a prelude
to when the mind will
be independent from the body.
We brew images to dwell in
ecstasy or nightmare when
consciousness is on its own.

My dentist says I grind my teeth
in my sleep.
Like gnashing of the teeth in Hell?
My dentist has made a mold
of my mouth.
The lab will mail me a mouth guard.
This will protect me from my dreams
for now.

The Devil is Getting Old

No more rebellion in heaven
No more Morning Star
No more trying to be God
The devil is getting old

No more hooves on rooftops
No more licking flames
No more slam dancing against bone
The devil is getting old

No more leather wings
No more flutes on hillsides
No more betting against the odds
The devil is getting old

No more riding waves of eyes
No more Jesus naked hippie cult
No more playing the record backwards
The devil is getting old

No more spiraling ram's horn to oblivion
No more going stag into the herd
Just moaning stalagmites of memory
The devil is getting old

As he sulks at the center
As he scratches his bristled balls
As he is crowned with shadow
The devil is getting old

Minions whisper that the surface
is ripe with war, famine, orgies of blood,
but he'd rather just stay in tonight
The devil is getting old

People are gullible, stupid, vain, but
let them be. We're all so lost.
He doesn't play with the souls he already has
The devil is getting old

He's got an altar of skulls he's fucked
Now he's resting on his nut
Deflated, a has been, a never was
The devil is getting old

He ain't angry anymore
He's blown off the steam that
fuels God's damnation machine
The devil is getting old

These days humanity is evil all by itself
They don't need him anymore
The student has become the master
The devil is getting old

He's sick of tricks
He's sick of masks
He wants you to know the real him
The devil is getting old

He's sick of running
He's ready to face the music
Would they dare forgive, forgive even him?
The devil is getting old

No more eyes aglow
No more fiery furnace passion
Just this heart frozen in ice
The devil is getting old

As he spins in space
As he grins a crescent moon
Free at last, alone in the void
The devil just wants to go home

About the Author: Reverse Route 66

Radio towers blink like red fireflies across the Texas Panhandle. Neurons sputter memories in the rearview mirror. Days ago I had a last drink with my wife on the patio of the Thirsty Crow on the Sunset Strip. Then one last kiss goodbye. Everything else has been said. Everything else has been tried. All my things were packed in a rental car a few blocks away on a hill with the emergency brake on. The car sagged full of books stacked in beer boxes scavenged from the corner liquor store.

As I fled, Los Angeles never seemed so inky. The sunset bled in the rearview. Shadows slithered ahead. Along the road the trees glowed in radioactive sap on the run being pursued by my past self. At 2 am I crashed with my old friend "Sailor" Scott in Arizona. After a few neat scotches I slept on his couch.

But my dreams scream. After years of writing for the muse I finally got a book deal. I was leaving an impossible situation in Hollywood, but at the same time my novel got picked up. You know the old saying: Every time God closes a door he farts and opens a window. My novel takes place in Chicago. It made sense to do readings there and stoke the hometown pride. Here I am tracing Route 66 back east. Traditionally driving Route 66 is to head to brighter times in sunny California. I've always been a contrary. Here I am swimming upstream again.

Then the desert outside Santa Fe with friends lined along the ridge painting the primordial horizon. Artist Daniel Stine and I visited Los Alamos a town on top of a mesa where the A-bomb was invented in the 1940s,

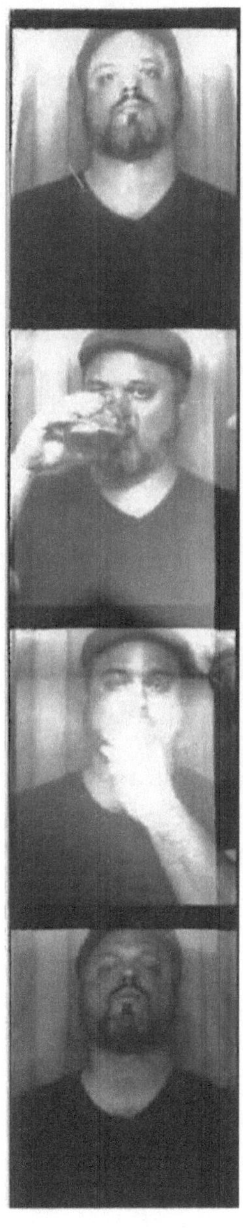

and where William Burroughs lost his cherry when it was a Boy Scout camp in the 1920s.

Now I'm crossing the Texas Panhandle. The classic rock fades from all the FM stations and all that remains are the religious channels. Finally I luck into a public station playing vintage blues. Robert Johnson sings Sweet Home Chicago. By the time the program is over my eyes are burnt out and my hands are shaking from the steering column vibrating at 85 mph. I stop at a roadhouse to have a beer. I watch honkytonk angels dancing and swirling like flowers in a stream.

In Shamrock Texas, I pull off to an ancient Route 66 motel. It's windswept as a 1980s slasher flick. Ringing the buzzer I awake an old Indian woman. I'm the only guest. She seems surprised to see me. $60 in cash and she shows me a room full of little piles of dust from the termites spitting tobacco. She turns on the heater that has been dead for a year. Musky ghosts howl through the room blowing dustbowl dreams.

Finally alone I sip the moonshine I had stashed in the trunk. I start feeling hot. I turn off the heater. I strip down.

The neon sign blinks around the edge of the shade. I examine myself in the tarnished mirror.

When did I get so old? I feel like a time traveler. Here I am lost in the future. 2022? I never thought I would live this long. Here I am. I'm turning forty. My skin is pale except for the beat red face blushing the alcoholic halo. My capillaries are bursting especially where the scar tissue from fights and accidents turn a deeper red. My beer belly hatches forth from under my rib cage and eclipses my dick, which once looked proportionate to my beefy body, but now sits like an afterthought under this gut protruding like a pale moon.

Laughing I dance naked before the mirror. It's a cracked memory, an illusion in reverse. I'm in the middle middle middle of America in the middle middle of life. Who would drive along Route 66 from California back to Chicago as winter begins? Robert Johnson singing Sweet Home Chicago echoes in my ear. Give me that cold hard truth. Give me the blues. Give me the facts of life. Give me the city that keeps it real.

Storm clouds are on the horizon. Dictators, fascists, and wars are popping up around the globe. It seems unreal that humans follow the herd in circles regurgitating history. Like vultures we chew carrion and puke it into the aching mouths of our children. What fun.

In Missouri I crash with some poets in an art collective, a residency commune where a foundation cleared out some meth-head houses. The town has reluctantly replaced speed freaks with artists. Us poets are a shade up from tweakers. After the reading I pull out my guitar on a midnight porch. Words wet the stars.

In the morning heaven burns my eyes. Fall leaves blow in psychedelic cyclones. I look at what's left of my bottle of Everclear. I decide that I no longer need to put flammable things in my body. I leave the bottle of grain alcohol on the communal table for the poets in case their writing starts to make too much sense. I leave a note: Don't drink this all at once. It will kill you.

The streets of St. Louis flow in red brick boulevards steady as the Mississippi down to the cemetery where William S. Burroughs is laid to rest. Fumbling by the gate the graveyard map (full of respectable citizens) doesn't mention naughty old Uncle Bill. An old black security guard approaches me. He knows my type. He knows the plot. He smiles and I follow him to where Burroughs finally got some peace after his long maddening life. Golden fall leaves blow in violent gusts around his stone. Wind! Wind! Wind! Right Bill? Uncle Bill, please give me the strength like you to live alone. Give me the strength to live for the work.

On to Chicago: Haven't been here since before the COVID-19 pandemic, since Obama was the President. I am a time traveler. I am from the past. For every plastic condo popping up like a mushroom cloud destroying my nostalgia for the bad old days I see ten businesses that have survived the storm. My people. I'm back. I'm back. I'm stronger than when I left. Home sweet home. Sweet home Chicago, right Robert Johnson? As the song goes, "To the land of California, sweet home Chicago." Despite the time-flak, despite the whiplash I am back. Back to work. Let's party like it's '99, like Route 66 in reverse.

Publication Notes

"I See You," "Booster," and "Bullfight at the Supermarket" were previously published in *Black Noise* April 2024 issue.

"My Old Lady" was previously published in *Tickets to Midnight Vol. 2* from Pure Sleeze Press.

"Zen in Hell" was previously published in *Letters For The End Times Vol. I* from Collapse Press.

"Shadowboxing in Uptown" was previously published in *Alien Buddha Zine #49*.

"Shot of Mercy" was previously published by Pure Sleeze Press.

"I Found Jesus" was previously published in *Down In The Dirt* from Scars Publications.

"You're Lite" was previously published in *Night Owl Narrative Issue No. 2 February 2024* from Cajun Mutt Press.

"Easy Street" was previously published as Chapter 27 in the novella *Picture Book* from Page Telegram Press & Westley Heine.

"Purgatory Diary" and "The Pterodactyl Cult" was previously published in *Letters For The End Times Vol. II* from Collapse Press.

"The Sphinx of Silverton" was previously published in *God, Guns, Glory, & Greed* from Dumpster Fire Press.

"Uptown Eddie" was previously published in *Tickets to Midnight Vol. 3* from Pure Sleeze Press.

"Honky Tonk Angels" was previously published in *Big Hammer issue #24.*

MORE ROADSIDE PRESS TITLES

By Plane, Train or Coincidence
Michele McDannold

Prying
Jack Micheline, Charles Bukowski and Catfish McDaris

Wolf Whistles Behind the Dumpster
Dan Provost

Busking Blues: Recollections of a Chicago Street Musician and Squatter
Westley Heine

Unknowable Things
Kerry Trautman

How to Play House
Heather Dorn

Kiss the Heathens
Ryan Quinn Flanagan

St. James Infirmary
Steven Meloan

Street Corner Spirits
Westley Heine

A Room Above a Convenience Store
William Taylor Jr.

Resurrection Song
George Wallace

Nothing and Too Much to Talk About
Nancy Patrice Davenport

Bar Guide for the Seriously Deranged
Alan Catlin

Born on Good Friday
Nathan Graziano

Under Normal Conditions
Karl Koweski

The Dead and the Desperate
Dan Denton

Clown Gravy
Misti Rainwater-Lites

Walking Away
Michael D. Grover

All in a Pretty Little Row
Dan Provost

These Are the People in Your Neighbourhood
Jordan Trethewey

They Said I Wasn't College Material
Scot Young

Radio Water
Francine Witte

And Blackberries Grew Wild
Susan Mickelberry

Licorice Heart
Miles Budimir

Disposable Darlings
Todd Cirillo

Full Moon Midnight
Belinda Subraman

Innocent Postcards
John Pietaro

Cistern Latitudes
James Duncan

Another Saturday Night in Jukebox Hell
Alan Catlin

Abandoned By All Things
Karl Koweski

Ain't These Sorrows Sweet?
Lauren Scharhag

Gregory Corso: Ten Times a Poet
Edited by Leon Horton

She Throws Herself Forward to Stop the Fall
Dave Newman

We Don't Get to Write the Ending
Aleathia Drehmer

These Many Cold Winters of the Heart
Ryan Quinn Flanagan

Things You Never Knew Existed
Josh Olsen

Maze
Jennifer Juneau

Green Roses Bloom for Icarus
Hiromi Yoshida

Let the Scaffolds Fall
Shaun Rouser

Apocalypsing
Jason Anderson

Failing to Fall
James Griffin

Last Bacchanale
George Wallace

Thrift Store Jackets
Karl Koweski

Night Bird Flying
Danny Shot

All Skate: True Stories from Middle Life
Lori Jakiela